A

Charming

Cure

Magical Cures Mystery Series

Book two

Also by Tonya Kappes

Women's Fiction
Carpe Bead 'em

Anthologies
Something Spooky This Way Comes
Believe Christmas Anthology

Olivia Davis Paranormal Mystery Series
Splitsville.com (Book One)

Magical Cures Mystery Series
A Charming Crime
A Charming Cure

Grandberry Falls Series
The Ladybug Jinx
Happy New Life
A Superstitious Christmas
Never Tell Your Dreams

A Divorced Diva Beading Mystery Series

A Bead of Doubt

Non-Fiction

The Tricked-Out Toolbox~Promotional and Marketing
Tools Every Writer Needs

What others are saying about Author Tonya Kappes

"Full of wit, humor and colorful characters, Tonya Kappes delivers a fun, fast-paced story that will leave you hooked!" Bestselling Author, Jane Porter

"Fun, fresh, and flirty, Carpe Bead 'Em is the perfect read on a hot summer day. Tonya Kappes' voice shines in her debut novel." Author Heather Webber

"I loved how Tonya Kappes was able to bring her characters to life." Coffee Table Reviews

With laugh out loud scenes and can't put it down suspense A Charming Crime is the perfect read for summer you get a little bit of everything but romance. Forgetthehousework blog

"This book was fun, entertaining and good to the last page. Who knew reading auras could get Olivia in so much trouble? Sit back, smile and cozy up to Splitsville.com, where Olivia does the dumping for you. There's heap loads of humor, a dose of magical realism, sprinkles of romance,

Dedication and Acknowledgments

I want to thank every single member of the Tonya Kappes Street Team! They are a group of readers who have stood by me and supported me. Readers are so important to me and I'm honored that at the end of the day they take the time to escape into my imaginative world. You guys rock!! AND I love you to death!

And to reader and friend, Amy Becker for winning the contest to name a character in A Charming Cure Name the Character contest. Raven is the perfect name for this new character in The Magical Cures Series.

Thank you, Judy Beatty, for turning my work into a polished work. Your talent is greatly amazing.

Of course a big magical hugs to my guys, Eddy, Jack, Austin, and Brady. They never complained once when we had take-out for the tenth day in a row while I completed this novel.

and mystery when someone ends up dead!" Author Lisa Lim

"This book was funny and clever with a unique premise. I truly couldn't put it down." Author Diane Majeske

"I loved this book. Grandberry Falls is my kind of town and I for one would love to live there and get to know all the local folks. I enjoyed reading this book and can't wait to read the next book about Grandberry Falls by Tonya Kappes. I have added Tonya Kappes as one of my new favorite authors." Jean Segal

"This was the first of a great new fantasy series. At first, I was a bit confused as to what was going on, but so was the main character, June, so I got to discover things right along with her, which I loved. As the mystery unfolded, and June learned more and more about herself, the fantasy world that Kappes introduced came to life. T is definitely one series that will be on my To Be Read l as subsequent books come out." author Andrea Bugin

Chapter One

"Bubble, bubble." My hands hovered over the copper cauldron, I leaned back. It was the first time I had ever used it and was a little unsure of the effects. If something was going to fly out, I didn't want it to hit me. Plus, I didn't want the fertility potion I was making to hit me. My fertility was fine exactly the way it was . . .non-existent. A puff of relief escaped my lips when nothing out of the ordinary happened, causing my blunt bangs to fly up in the air.

I stood up straighter, pulled down the edges of my jean jacket and picked up the Magical Cures Book. Little did I realize that when my mother, Darla, left me the book in her last will and testament, it would teach me who I really was.

Slowly, I opened the leather bound book and found my page. I held it up to my nose. With a deep inhale, and with a bee fertility cure in mind, cinnamon, sage, yellow jasmine and Marsh tea took over my senses. I sat the book down next to the cauldron and placed my hands back over it.

Nothing happened so I continued. This time I spoke a little louder, "Bubble, bubble. Clear the bee's troubles. Let the bee's create honey, to keep bringing Petunia more money."

Steam flew upward as I pinched off different ingredients and tossed them in the simmering pot. Petunia peeked around the partition, making me a little nervous.

Originally, I had the cauldron in the back of A Charming Cure, but I didn't like going in the back and leaving the shop unattended. So, I had the counter made taller and a partition to block off any and all magic happening behind it.

I ducked as a mini-tornado whirled and churned like mad over the steam. Carefully, I reached over and threw in a dash of Marigold just like the instruction in the Magical Cures book said to do. Only it didn't say throw, it said to gently stir.

As soon as the Marigold flakes hit the bubbling water, sparks flew up, stopping the cylinder from twirling. The cauldron shut off, letting me know the bee-pollen potion was finished.

Petunia stepped back from the partition.

"Scardy-cat." I smiled and picked up the ladle, stirring the mixture and making sure it was the right consistency.

"I'll take licks and rubs over that any day," she chimed from the other side of the partition, referring to her four-legged creatures.

She owned Gollybee Pet Store a few shops down. Every shop owner in Whispering Falls had a psychic ability with a magical twist. The entire village was magical.

To an outsider, Whispering Falls, Kentucky was just a tiny town with a population of five hundred, set in the foothills of a few mountains. Most people that visited our little village didn't know how special we really were, but they felt the magic while they were here, which was why they continued to come back for more.

Meow, meow. Mr. Prince Charming ran over and created figure eights around her ankles. You could always tell when my cat liked you. He would do his signature figure eight move.

The bell above the door dinged, letting me know that my first customer of the day was here. I glanced up at the clock. There was still five minutes until A Charming Cure opened, but I would never turn someone away that needed a cure for whatever ailed them.

"Good morning, Mr. Prince Charming." In one quick move, Petunia picked up the cat. Her hazel eyes narrowed and focused on the customer. Petunia pushed the stick back in place that was falling out of her makeshift up-do she had created with her long, brown hair. She always had some sort of nature hanging around in there. Sometimes it was a small creature, but today it was a twig. Petunia's gift was being able to communicate with animals and Mr. Prince Charming loved her.

"I'll be right with you." I popped my head around the partition and stared at the woman dressed in all black. I tucked my black bob haircut behind my ear, and pushed my blunt bangs to the side to get a better look. She didn't look like one of my usual customers.

Without acknowledging me or without a word, the woman's long, thin hand stretched out and retrieved a homeopathic bottle from the round, tiered table that sat just inside the door.

Hiss, hiss. Mr. Prince Charming had jumped out of Petunia's arms and stood at attention facing the customer. He was never good at disguising his dislikes either.

"Mr. Prince Charming!" I whistled him over, and he came running behind the counter. "I'm so sorry. I'll be right with you."

Quickly I grabbed the glass bottle that looked like a stack of lifesavers. The rainbow-inspired bottle lit up when I touched it, letting me know it was the perfect match for the bee pollen. I put a small funnel in the mouth of the bottle. I scooped the potion in the ladle and carefully poured it into the funnel. Slowly, the potion dripped into the bottle. I twisted the lid on securely and waited until it was ready.

Meow, meow. Mr. Prince Charming jumped up and landed next to the box of Ding Dongs.

"You know exactly what I need." Carefully, I unwrapped the foil and took a big bite of what I considered to be real magic. The chocolate treat was magic to my soul. The best comfort food—ever! My go-to when I became stressed. And, for some odd reason, the new customer seemed to put my intuition on high alert.

That was my psychic gift. I didn't have anything cool like the mediums, palm readers, and tarot readers of the village. But, my intuition had never failed me, so I guess it was a good gift to have, even though I sometimes wish I could turn a few people into ants or fleas.

I pinched a small piece off and fed it to him. I'd always heard chocolate wasn't good for animals, but fifteen years of eating Ding Dongs hadn't hurt him yet. He'd *never* been to the veterinarian. I tried taking him a few times in Locust Grove, Kentucky, where we lived before we moved to Whispering Falls, but somehow he'd end up disappearing right before my eyes. Finally, I gave up.

The bee pollen glowed in the rainbow bottle. It was ready.

"All done." I held the bottle in the palm of my hand and walked out from behind the partition. "Just add a few drops to the hive and you'll be buzzing with babies in no time. Pun intended." A big smile crept up on my face.

I was the youngest and newest spiritualist in the community and I was sure they still didn't know how to take the Samantha Stevens wannabe.

Petunia didn't smile at my joke. She took the bottle, but never took her eyes off the customer who continued to pick up my bottles while curling her nose.

The customer had picked up the lime green potion bottle that was sitting on the corner shelf closest to the door. Tapping the bottle with her red-tipped fingernail, her eyebrows raised.

"Do I know you?" There was something familiar about her. At least that was what my intuition told me, and it wasn't in favor of her. Before I gave her a not-so-nice potion, say a potion that would turn her hiccups into a croaking frog or her negative attitude into one of giving, I needed to know her answer.

It was only a few weeks or so ago that I moved to Whispering Falls, Kentucky, took over Darla's, my deceased mom's, homeopathic shop, and made it my own. After the initial shock from learning that my father had psychic abilities as a healer by using cures, I'd became excited to learn that I too had inherited the psychic gene. A Charming Cure had taken off.

Not only was I dishing up the best homeopathic cure, I was also giving a little extra dose of magic in each potion. Also, I had a knack for knowing what else someone needed in their life. A little extra dose of love or a little financial help didn't hurt anyone. My intuition never let me down.

Hiss, Hiss. Mr. Prince Charming, my cat, darted out from the counter. *Hiss, Hiss.* He pawed the air with his back arched and his teeth gnashing toward the woman.

"Oh, shut up!" She drew her black cloak around her as if she was shielding an attack from Mr. Prince Charming. "I should've squashed you when you were a kitten. I had plenty of opportunities when I fed you."

"Are you his owner?" No way! There was no way I was going to give Mr. Prince Charming back to his original owner. Especially someone that seemed to be as nasty as her. "I've taken really good care of him over the last fifteen years. I'd be happy to pay you for him."

Mr. Prince Charming was unlike any other stray cat in Locust Grove, the town I grew up in before I moved to Whispering Falls. There were a lot of stray cats. He showed up on my porch on what-so-happened-to-be my tenth birthday. He had on a faded collar with a tiny turtle charm dangling off it. The turtle had one green emerald stone for an eye and the other one missing. I didn't care. It was beautiful.

Oscar, my childhood best friend and now Whispering Falls sheriff, had asked around if the cat belonged to anyone. No one claimed him, and he just continued to hang around. Darla didn't mind, so he stayed. I got him a new collar and kept the charm for myself.

"Want him back?" She threw her head back letting out a full cackle that rattled the bottles on the shelf. "Oh, no. I don't want him back. I'm here to collect you." The woman raised her voice. Petunia rushed between us and came nose to nose with her. The scary woman continued, "She has no choice. She must leave right now!"

"Take me?" My mouth dried, and I gasped for air. Water filled my eyes. "Take me where?"

Petunia turned toward me, embracing me. She whispered in my ear, "its okay, June."

"What is okay?" The room spun around me. Things definitely weren't okay.

"This is your Great Aunt Helena," Petunia whispered as if it was going to ease the blow. "She's the Dean at Hidden Hall A Spiritualist University. The school for people like . . . *us*." She fanned her hands in the air.

"School? Hidden Hall? " This really shouldn't have come as a surprise because Whispering Falls was definitely full of them, but I never thought I'd be going back to school, especially to hone my magical skills. "Listen, I'm *not* college material."

Didn't they realize that I went straight out of high school, selling Darla's potions at a *flea market*? Far from going to college.

Mewwwl, Mewwl, Mr. Prince Charming cried, and hung his head. His tail was not wagging as it normally did.

"I told you to shut-up. You know the rules!" A spark shot from Helena's eyes. "Quite frankly, I'm surprised you they let you stay here. What good were you? You let the killer live right across the street!"

Hiss, hiss. Mr. Prince Charming batted at the woman, claws out and ready to slash.

"What is going on here?" A clap of thunder gave way to an all out downpour outside just as the door opened and Isadora Solstice bolted in. Her hot pink A-line skirt swayed with each step she took in her pointy-toed black, laced-up boots. She stopped when she saw Aunt Helena. She folded her arms and spoke lightly, "Helena, we've been expecting you."

"We have?" My hands balled up into fists and dangled at my side. I certainly had not been expecting anyone. Especially a long lost member of my family.

Helena pointed at Mr. Prince Charming and scowled, "He is your fairy god-cat, who was supposed to take care of

you. And all he did was get you in a lot of hot water. Mr.
Prince Charming *my ass*."

"I . . . I," I stammered. The room spun faster. A Ding
Dong would taste good. I reached for the counter. Instead
of grabbing one, I grabbed the edge of the counter and held
on for dear life.

Petunia grabbed Mr. Prince Charming. "He did a fine
job. He gave you all those charms to protect and guide you.
See." She touched my wrist.

She was right. Mr. Prince Charming did steal several
charms from Belle's Baubles in Whispering Falls, but Belle
claimed they were presents from her. If I thought back a
little more, Mr. Prince Charming was always around when
I found myself in hot water, even was I was a kid.
Memories whipped around my head like the small funnel
clouds do when I mix a cure.

Everything started to add up. Mr. Prince Charming
really *had* been watching over me all these years.

"June." Izzy put her hands on my shoulders.
"Remember how good souls come back as animals?"

I nodded, my mind cloudy.

"Well, your father couldn't come back as an animal
because he was married to your mom, a mortal. But, your

grandparents were pillars of the village so we were delighted when they appointed a fairy god-cat to watch over you. You know, in case something happened to your parents." She picked him up and stroked his back. White fur flew everywhere.

Helena swooped across the floor and created a breeze when her cloak wrapped around her. She stopped in front of me. I pushed my blunt black bangs out of my eyes. She obviously had more magic in her one pinky than I had in my entire shop. Now she had the type of magic I wished I had. Not just a little dab of this or a dollop of that.

"It's time, June." She held her hand out for me to take. "I'm here to collect my niece."

I reached out, but hesitated. This was all still new to me and I had learned to just believe in what went on around me in Whispering Falls. I pulled my hand back.

"I'm not joking, June." A spark flew from her finger. "It's time to go."

Chapter Two

No one seemed to want to argue with Helena but me. Mr. Prince Charming seemed to be stunned. He sat motionless in front of the shop door, no dragging tail, no figure-eights… just staring at her.

"He's my fairy god-cat?" I knew it. I looked to Petunia for some answers. "Can you talk to him?"

"He is a fairy god-cat. He didn't come back from the dead like the animals that I talk to do." She rushed over; leaves fell out of her beehive of a hair-do and onto the floor. She gave Mr. Prince Charming a good rub under his chin. "He's done a fine job. He continues to do exactly what he was supposed to do." She turns and glares toward Aunt Helena.

"Fine." Helena rolled her eyes and let out a big sigh. "Regardless. All of you know that every new village member has to go to school. It just so happen that it's my heir this time. And we all know what *that* means."

"*I* don't know what *that* means!" There was a nervous tickle in my stomach. Mr. Prince Charming ran over and did figure eights around my ankles. He knew actually what I needed, his reassurance that I was going to be okay.

"It means that you will tap even further into your spiritual gift. You might even have another ability you don't know about." She drew her cloak close to her.

Hmm . . . so, I might just *be* a little Samantha Stevens? Or maybe have cool magical and psychic abilities like the Fairiwicks.

"You are not a Fairiwick." Her eyes were icy and unresponsive.

Did she just read my mind? I eyed her suspiciously. *You're a whack job,* I hoped she read that thought too, but she didn't flinch.

Fairiwicks were bred of spiritualists that were half fairy and half witches. Just recently, the village council approved Fairiwicks to join the community. Before that, only psychics lived in Whispering Falls.

"We are an inter-communal village now." Izzy's eyes narrowed, zeroing in on Helena.

"Umm, hmm. I heard." Helena pursed her lips. Disgust dripped in her voice. "In my day. . ."

"We aren't *in* your day." There was a confidence building in me that I couldn't explain.

If what she was saying was true, my grandparents were the royalty of the village, leaving my father as the heir. Of course, I wasn't here to take over, so it went to my Great Aunt Helena. I was here now.

"You are a smart one." Helena crossed her arms in front of her. "You have to go to school. Your father would expect it. Besides, it's a rule. See section F in the village handbook."

Oh, throwing in the family card?

"Just how well did you know my father?" It was a valid question. If she was such a wonderful Aunt and cared for my well-being, where was she when I was framed for murder a few months ago?

I admit that I had not read all the way through the rule book that Izzy had given me when I moved to Whispering Falls. All I knew was that there was a village council that included Izzy, Gerald Reguila, Chandra Shango, and Petunia Sandlewood.

"And one day, we were hoping you could take over as council President." Izzy brushed her long wavy blonde hair behind her shoulders away from her face, revealing her beautiful hazel eyes.

Petunia bent down and picked Mr. Prince Charming up. "Everyone loves your sweet nature and fresh presence. You would make a very popular village council President."

Council President? This situation was getting weirder by the minute.

"I'm getting old, June, and we need fresh voices." Izzy's chest heaved in and out with each breath. "And Helena is right. You do have to go to school in order to make the cures. You have only lightly tapped into your psychic powers."

Tapped? Knowing how to make cures with my intuition was enough power for me. But what would happen if I did have some cool power I didn't know about? I admit I was a magic wannabe.

"Do I have to go away to school?" There was no way I wanted to leave A Charming Cure or Whispering Falls. I was just getting use to the move and embracing the village. Plus, business was booming. The extra income was exactly what I needed to buy more ingredients to produce more products. Especially for the made-to-order customers. Some of those required ingredients from all over the world.

"It's preferable, especially if you are going to be the Village president." Helena pushed back her auburn hair exposing a scar that started at her ear and ran along her jaw line. Quickly she pulled her hair over her shoulder when she saw me staring at it. "Or you can go to the two-day quick class with a few of the chosen."

"What if I don't want to be President?" I didn't run for any office when I was in high school, much less President of an entire village. "Besides, I'm too old to go to a University"

Anticipation and excitement lay like a lump in my throat as they all stared at me like I had five heads, which really wouldn't be that unusual in a spiritualist community.

"Okay fine." I inhaled, not believing what just came out of my mouth. Going to college was something I wasn't cut out for, but maybe I could just do my four days and be done with it.

Izzy smiled and clasped her hands together. "Thank you, June." She tilted her head towards Helena, and a wide smile covered her face. "Since that is settled, why don't you come to The Gathering Grove and visit with Gerald?"

"Well, I could use a real cup of tea. Hidden Hall can't seem to serve a decent cup. Which is odd, since we have so many tea leaf readers going to school." Helena's attitude had made a complete 180 degree turn. "And it would be good to catch up with old University friends."

The two of them headed toward to the door.

"Oh, he will be delighted to see you, and laugh about old times." Izzy put her hand on the door, and then glanced around. "June? Petunia? Are you going to join us?"

Petunia held the bee pollen potion in the air. "No. I have some bee issues to take care of."

I shook my head. "No, I had better settle a few things here before I go on my mini-school trip."

"Don't worry about A Charming Cure. We will make sure it's taken care of." Izzy held the door open and swept her hand in front of her and said, "After you, Helena."

Once out the door, Helena looked back in the shop. "Oh, June, there are no electronics allowed at Hidden Hall. You must rely on your own abilities and not the abilities of Mr. Google or a cell phone. You'd be surprised on how many students would cheat that way. I'll see you tomorrow, June."

"Tomorrow." I nervously smiled. There was something about tomorrow that didn't sit well, which gave me bit of a worry. When something didn't "sit well," that meant my intuition was trying to tell me something. Only I didn't have time to listen to it. I had limited time to tell Oscar goodbye and talk him into looking after the shop while I was gone.

Chapter Three

"Okay, spill it." I watched Helena and Izzy get reacquainted as they walked down the street to The Gathering Grove Tea Shoppe. "What is my *Aunt Helena* all about?" Saying Aunt Helena made my eyes roll.

"You know I don't do idle gossip. " Petunia peeked out the window and watched them. "But I can tell you that Gerald isn't going to be happy to see her."

I made a mental note to ask Gerald about his history with Helena since Petunia wasn't going to give in it idle gossip. A few customers came in the door.

"Welcome to A Charming Cure. Let me know if I can mix up a homeopathic cure for what ails you." Immediately I knew what ailed the blond. Deep down I knew it wasn't the big zit sitting on the edge of her pointy nose that was her problem. The tall blonde politely smiled and nodded.

I motioned for Petunia to follow me to the counter and let the customers look around. Usually it took new customers a while to mosey around and see what the store was all about. I always give them a little time before I draw out what they came in for.

"Hmm. . .if she is my aunt and so concerned about me, why didn't she come to my rescue when the entire town accused me of killing Ann?" It was a valid question. And it would've been nice to have had a living relative back me up when someone had framed me.

I smiled at the blonde who looked up after glancing over the facial remedies of the shop.

"She's keeping a secret," I whispered to Petunia about the blonde customer with the zit. "I wonder".

"Huh! Wonder about what?" Petunia looked up her up and down.

I shrugged. "I don't know, but I know she's torn over it. Let's get back to Aunt Helena." I knew Petunia had some information about why Gerald wasn't going to be happy to see her. After all, she and Gerald had been dating on the down-low for the last few months.

"Gerald did say that he knew she was going to come because he happened to read Izzy's tea leaves when she left the other day." Petunia's hand flew over her mouth as her brows rose. "But I'm not gossiping."

"Oh, I know you aren't." I shook my head, knowing good and well she was dying to tell me.

"And the leaves said. . ." she proceeded with caution in her voice until she was interrupted.

"Excuse me," The blonde woman walked up. "I need a little help."

Damn! I put my finger up to Petunia, and said, "Hold that thought."

I wasn't going to let her forget what she was going to say. I needed to know what the tea leaves said and I needed to know all about Helena. There was something fishy with her and I wanted to know everything I could before I went to Hidden Hall A Spiritualist University.

"What can I do for you?" I rubbed my hands together. I wasn't sure how I was going to draw the truth out of her. Fact was, I already knew from my intuition that she was harboring a secret that needed to come out. Hence the zit. Stress does wonders on the body.

"I was looking at your facial remedies and there doesn't seem to be anything specific for zits." She walked over to the beautiful glass bottles that were displayed on the shelving in the middle of the store. She tapped the tip of her nose. "I've been having a little acne issue for a couple months."

Ahh. So, she's been keeping this secret for a couple months.

"I see." Lightly, I ran my fingers along the front of the bottles trying to decide how to handle the situation. Just asking could work. "Has something changed in your life to make you stressed?"

"Nope. Nothing." She shook her head so fast; I thought it was going to spin off. She stepped back and looked away.

There was no way I was going to get the truth from her, but the real remedy would.

"And are you getting a cluster of pimples or just one at a time?" I let her presence take over my gut, my senses. I had to know exactly what she was feeling in order to get the right cure, and it wasn't for zits.

"It's the strangest thing." She picked up a couple different bottles to check out the label. Her energy started to surround the two of us, and I got a good feeling about the truth brewing inside her. "I get one *big* one every week, and then it goes away before the next one."

Yep, a sure secret keepers sign. I rolled up on my toes just a little to get a better look, but the eyes told the story.

Her secret was deep rooted and she needed a stronger remedy than normal.

"Hmm. . ." I glanced at the bottles one more time, pretending to see if there was a cure, but I knew I was going to have to make one with a little extra something-something in it. "I'm all out of the particular one you need."

Worry settled on her face.

"It'll only take me a moment to whip one up." I lifted my finger to reassure her.

"Yes, please." Her blonde hair flung around as she nodded.

"Great. I'll be right back." I turned to go make the perfect cure for acne and a dose of the truth. Plus, making the remedy would give me more time to pick Petunia's brain about Gerald reading Izzy's tea leaves, even though it was against council rules to read any spiritualist without the spiritualist knowing. One thing I did know, Izzy would never let anyone, and especially not Gerald, read her.

Glancing around the shop as I hid behind the partition, I didn't see Petunia. Quickly I looked in the back where I keep a mini-refrigerator and couch for those 'just-in-case I stay later than normal' nights, but she wasn't in there.

Mr. Prince Charming followed.

"Hmm. . .She must've left. How convenient." I walked back to the counter and prepared myself to make the customer's cure.

Meow, meow. Mr. Prince Charming jumped on the counter. A small silver owl charm dropped from his mouth.

Oh, no. My heart fell into my newly pedicure toes. My intuition told me this wasn't a good sign. Mr. Prince Charming was good at "stealing" charms that had the meaning of protection. And it just so happened that when he did give me a charm, it was when I needed extra safe keeping.

I rubbed my hand down his back, and then pushed the charm to the side. It was going to have to wait until I could see Belle from Belle's Baubles to figure out if he stole it and what the owl meant.

I reached into the Ding Dong box and grabbed one.

The customer milled around, picking up the bottles and reading the contents. She looked over when I unwrapped the foil on my chocolaty treat and took a bite.

"It's almost done." I smiled with the round, dark goodness stuck to the front of my teeth.

Truth be told, I hadn't even begun to make her cure. With a big bite in my mouth, I flipped the cauldron on high.

I reached on the shelf for the sack of Antmonuin to help with her skin condition. I carefully untied the drawstring bag, and took a pinch of it. I threw it in the cauldron and watched the liquid froth.

"Eh, a little more?" I shrugged and looked at Mr. Prince Charming.

Meow.

That was enough of a yes from him to throw in a couple more pinches. You can never have clear enough skin.

Gently stirring counter clockwise, the liquid became a murky pink color. Steam rolled up, leaving a smell of peach in the air.

"Now for the good stuff," I whispered and shivered with excitement.

My newly found abilities were still fresh and exciting.

Carefully I picked a bloom from the Land Kelp plant and tossed it in. Slowly I hovered my hands above the cauldron clockwise causing the mixture to change directions and thinning out the mixture and color.

"Mmm…I love peach," the customer hollered from the sleeping remedies side of the store. "What smells like peaches?"

She snapped me out of my focus. I peeped my head around the partition, and said, "I'll be right with you."

Little did she realize, that when I make a particular potion for someone in mind, somehow the potion takes on flavors and smells the recipient loves, making the potion a wonderful disguise for what it was really meant to do. And in her case. . .the truth shall set you free…of stress and zits.

I returned back to the cauldron and smiled, wondering how the customer was going to feel about the peach smell but the cucumber taste.

The cauldron shut off, leaving the glowing pink mixture simmering at a slow bubble.

The red and gold glass bottle on the far end of the empty glass bottle shelf, glowed, letting me know it was the perfect container for this particular potion. Unscrewing the delicate triangular lid, I held the bottle down into the liquid. Instantly, the potion cooled and seeped into the bottle. Sparks flew up and bounced off the ceiling and landed on top of the customer's head.

A patch of her blonde hair turned charcoal and a puff of smoke rose from it.

Oh crap! I bit the edge of my lip. I wasn't responsible for the sparks, or at least I hoped I wasn't.

"How much longer?" She looked up and asked. The smoke changed directions with each turn of her head. She was either unfazed or unaware that she was emitting smoke. "I've got to get home. I feel a sudden urge to tell my best-friend her no-good-for-nothing husband is cheating on her with her own cousin!"

She let a big sigh of relief as if a ton of bricks was lifted off her shoulders.

And there was the secret. Just like magic, the zit on the edge of her nose disappeared.

"All done." I held the bottle up and ran over to her before she could catch her reflection in one of the hanging mirrors in the shop. I put a dab of liquid on my finger and touched her nose. "Now, don't look in the mirror until you get home."

"But I thought I was supposed to drink it." She eyed me. "Oh, well. How much do I owe?"

She followed me back to the other side of the counter where the cash register was. On a scrap piece of paper, I wrote out the receipt and handed it to her.

"I love your shop." She smiled, handing me the cash and walked out waving bye over her shoulder, just as Oscar Park held the door for her with his foot while juggling two coffees.

"Good morning, June." He held his gaze and flashed his million-dollar smile.

No! My heart fluttered the closer he got. His clear blue eyes locked with mine, sending chills up my legs. *Look away, look away.* But I couldn't. For the past couple of months, something unusual was happening to my feelings toward my childhood best friend.

Meowl. Mr. Prince Charming let out one long sigh.

Oscar grew up across the street from me and Darla in Locust Grove. Overnight he went from being awkwardly scrawny, to hunky handsome. Especially after he saved me from a murderer's hand our first week in Whispering Falls. Another story for another time, but I was sure that was when it had happened.

What woman didn't like to be rescued? I questioned, taking in his freshly cut black hair that was perfectly short. Plus, he looked great in a Whispering Falls police uniform.

"What's that?" I pointed to the new accessory on his belt, while taking a cup of coffee from him with the other hand.

His eyes lit up and he took out the small stick that was too small to be a Billy club. He flipped it up in the air, caught it and waved it around. "My sorcerer's wand."

Oscar and I had found out at the same time that we were both from spiritualist families. Mine was boring psychic, while he was a cool Fairiwick.

"Wow!" I reached out to touch it, but he pulled it away.

"No touchy!" He put it back in the holster.

My intuition told me that he wasn't sure how to work it, but I wasn't going to ask him. "I'm glad you are here. I need a favor."

*Prrr. . . .*Mr. Prince Charming purred as he jumped down and did his signature figure eight move around Oscar's ankles.

I told him about Aunt Helena and Hidden Hall A Spiritual University . "I'm sure you'll be going." I informed him and left out all the 'how they want me to become Village president' one day details. I didn't understand it enough to even explain it. "Here's my favor," I took a deep breath and continued, "I need you to work the shop while I'm gone for my four days of school."

It was a tall order. But how difficult could it be to sell the items that were already on the shelf. I wasn't asking him to make any potions. If there was an emergency, he could ask Izzy. After all, what could happen in four days?

"What?" The sip of coffee he took sprayed out and down, all over Mr. Prince Charming.

Hiss, hiss. Mr. Prince Charming ran out the cat door that Oscar had installed in the front door of the shop.

"It's not like you can't do both jobs. Whispering Falls is not a crime-ridden city," I reminded him; unless he wanted to count the fact that he had just solved the murder of one of the village members. But that was water under the bridge. . .or so I hoped.

"I can't mix a cocktail, much less a potion." Oscar laughed, his eyes dancing. His smile faded when he realized I wasn't kidding. "Oh, you aren't kidding."

"No I'm not." Silence loomed like a heavy mist.

"You're not what?" Belle Vanlow questioned as she held the door for the last customer of the evening.

She was the closest to my and Oscar's age that lived in the community. Standing at five foot two, her blonde hair braided in two pigtails dangling below her round cheeks, made her look more like twelve years old instead of thirty.

"I asked Oscar to watch the shop while I'm gone to Hidden Hall." My eyes darted back and forth between the two.

She didn't question me, so I knew she had already heard the news of Helena and going to school.

"Yes, I heard about that." She flipped the open sign to closed, knowing it was time to shut down for the night, and then held up a pair of needle-nosed pliers. "I came by to put your new owl charm on your bracelet."

"That's my cue to leave." Oscar nodded toward the jewelry stuff. "June, I'll talk to you before you leave."

"Okay." I waved knowing, he would make good on his promise. He always did. That was one great personality trait about Oscar; he always kept his word.

Belle and I watched him leave.

"Yep, you seem to have a little something for him."
She grabbed my arm and unclasped my charm bracelet.
"And it doesn't take an astrologer to figure that out."

Belle was the astrologer in the community. Her
jewelry shop, Belle's Baubles, was a great place for her to
have all earthy elements and be able to read people's
stones. When a customer comes into the store, they think
they want a certain stone, but Belle knows the stone or
piece of jewelry that they really need and somehow talks
them into it. They always come back for more.

"Oscar and I are just good friends." *Hmm. . .*I admit
there did seem to be a little more interest but it was going
to have to wait. There would be no future if I didn't get
Hidden Hall out of the way and figure out what Petunia
heard from Gerald about my ever-so-endearing Aunt.

"Besides, there are a lot of things I still need to learn
about Whispering Falls and my abilities before I can bring
anyone else into my crazy life." I pulled a roll of paper
towels out from underneath the counter. I needed to finish
cleaning up for the night and have everything ready to go
for Oscar.

As Belle worked on putting the charm on my bracelet,
I rubbed the inside of the cauldron. As many times as I

have done this, there didn't seem to be a really good way to clean it.

"Those darn things never get good and clean do they?" She stopped to watch. Her pigtails swung in the pot. She grabbed them. Her fingernails were painted light blue with a tiny star in the middle.

"No matter what cleaning concoction I put together, I can never seem to get it all cleaned out." I gave up and put the tiny bottles of herbs back on the shelf. Belle followed my lead and helped. After we had them placed back in alphabetic order, I went down the shelves to make sure they were replenished.

I had no idea how it was done, but the bottles in A Charming Cure filled up as you put them in their rightful spot. I didn't care how the magic happened, I was just glad it did.

"Let's get back to Oscar and this information about him running the store." Belle put the bracelet back on my wrist.

I tucked the ends of my black bob behind my ears, and rubbed my hands down my apron before reaching around and untying the strings. "Let's not and say we did." I hung the apron on the hook on the wall next to the counter.

"I'm not talking about the love thing; I'm talking about how he is going to know what potions to make for the customer." Her eyes studied me with curiosity.

Back in Locust Grove where I ran A Dose of Darla out of a flea market booth after Darla had died, Oscar was with me day and night helping me make all sorts of cures out of the journal Darla had left me. Little did I know that it was the Magical Cures Book. However, the cure book only worked for me, since I had the spiritual gift of knowing what the real cure needed to be. If the book were stolen or someone else tried to make the cures in it, like Oscar, the cures would strictly be homeopathic with no extra umph in them.

"Oscar has been around me long enough to know what cures a sour stomach or a tooth ache." That was all Belle needed to know. "But if you could check on him every once in a while, that would be great. And, it's only four days. What can happen in four days?"

"You'd be surprised," She muttered under her breath.

Mewl, Mewl. Mr. Prince Charming stood on his hind legs and batted at the dangling bracelet.

"Oh, that reminds me," I jogged the bracelet up and down letting him play a little more. "What does the owl mean anyway?" It didn't seem like much of a protection charm like all the other ones that Mr. Prince Charming had given me.

"Umm. . ." She looked at Mr. Prince Charming. He did figure eights around her ankles. "It means wisdom. I think the protection behind it is to use your brains and everything you have learned here in Whispering Falls while you are at Hidden Hall."

Wisdom? If I were so wise, I wouldn't have to go to school.

Izzy and Helena caught my eye as they walked out of The Gathering Grove.

"Hey, let's go grab a cup of tea." There wasn't a better time to question Gerald than now, especially since Helena just saw him.

"Oh, I could use some Sleepy Time right now." Belle agreed and we closed and locked the shop up behind us.

The streets were still filled with some visitors getting in the last bit of shopping or spiritual advice. Even though people didn't know that Whispering Falls was magical, it was. And each shop owner added a little touch of advice or magic to their customers' purchases.

I looked into at A Cleansing Spirit Spa, which was next door to Charming Cure, when we walked by. Chandra Shango's turban was falling off her head as she worked on a customer's fingernails. The customer was taking in everything Chandra was telling her.

I smiled, knowing Chandra was giving her a bit of advice since she was a palm reader and spent more time on messaging their palm during the manicure than the nails themselves.

Golly Bee Pet Store was filled with customers and their animals. I could see the live tree that was inside the store was filled with all sorts of animals. They all got along. Petunia stood near the cash register with a squirrel on her shoulder as she talked to a bird that sat on top of the counter.

And then there was Izzy's shop, Mystic Lights. The sign was turned to closed so I was sure she was still with Helena. Izzy was a crystal ball reader and evidently, I was too. Mystic Lights was where Madame Torres came from. She glowed every time I went in to visit Izzy, and that was how Madame Torres picked me. You didn't pick your ball, or I wouldn't have the smart-alecky Madame Torres. Not that she wasn't great and didn't do her job, she did. But she gave me a hard time while doing it.

Finally, we made it down to The Gathering Grove, Gerald's tea shop. Mr. Prince Charming had already gone in.

"What's going in there?" I pointed to the empty shop space next to the tea shop. It was crazy. That wasn't there this morning. Things happen to appear and disappear in Whispering Falls with a blink of the eye.

"It must be a new shop." Belle put her nose up to the glass and covered her eyes so she could see in. "Looks like some sort of bakery."

I grabbed the handle of the Gathering Grove door and opened it for her to walk in. "Maybe Gerald is expanding since he has to drive to Locust Grove to get some of the pastries he sells."

Belle shrugged and walked on in.

"Good evening, ladies." Gerald took off his top hat and greeted us. "Seat yourself."

It was crowded. It was the only place in Whispering Falls to get any type of food. It was a popular destination for dessert and tea.

We scored a little table for three in the corner next to the window.

Gerald came over with a notepad in hand. "Some Sleepy Time for you ladies?"

"Not for me. I'll have a decaf and one of the red-velvet cupcakes." I couldn't get enough of those cupcakes. They had become really popular lately and it was showing on my thighs.

"I'll have some Sleepy Time and a red-velvet cupcake as well." Belle nodded.

"Coming right up." Gerald tapped the pad and went back to the counter to retrieve our order.

"You love sleepy time." Belle's eyes narrowed.

"Yes, but I leave early for school and I don't want to miss my alarm." I grabbed a napkin from the center of the table and put it in my lap when I saw Gerald coming with our food. He set the cupcakes and tea on the table.

"Sleepy Time for you. And a decaf for you." Gerald twirled his mustache when he was done. "Is there anything else I can get you?"

I really didn't want to do this in front of Belle, but I did anyway.

"Yes, can you sit down?" I pushed the chair out and patted it for him to sit. "I have a couple questions about Helena."

His eyes bulged from his head. I tried not to stare so I looked into my cup and noticed the floating tea leaves. I should've ordered it strained, because from what Petunia said, I knew he was reading spiritualist's leaves without them knowing. This was rule number one in the village rule book.

You aren't allowed to read spiritualists unless they give you permission. Gerald was a sly one.

"I. . .um. . .I don't know what you are talking about." Gerald cleared his throat. A sure sign he was lying.

"Gerald, you know and I know that you read Izzy's leaves and knew Helena was coming to town." I said, and then looked over at Belle when a squeak came out of her mouth. "Personally I don't care, but I do care when it has something to do with me. Helena has everything to do with me."

He leaned in and whispered, "Does this mean you are going to tell the village council since I'm already on trial for my relationship with Petunia?"

Belle smacked the table. The tea in the small china cups swayed back and forth to the rim, but never spilled over. "I knew it! I knew there was something going on between you two."

I planted my hand over her mouth. People were starting to stare at us.

"Shh. I'm not talking about that right now. I'm talking about Helena and Izzy." I took my hand away, and turned back to Gerald. "I'll make a deal with you. You tell me about the reading that only pertains to me and I will put in a good word about you and Petunia. Plus, I'll keep my mouth shut about you reading Izzy's leaves."

Without hesitation, Gerald stuck his hand over the table. "Deal."

We shook on it.

"Normally I don't read leaves, but for some strange reason I looked at Izzy's cup." He cleared his throat…again…*liar!* He talked while I looked down at the leaves in my tea. "There was a leaf in the shape of Hidden Hall and a letter 'H' next to it. But, there was a cluster of letters that I didn't understand. A 'U' and 'S.'" His eyes glowed as he told the reading. He was in the zone. "I got chills when I saw the cauldron with a cross bones and skull."

Something cautioned me not to interrupt him while he was remembering, but the words flew from my mouth, "Cauldron? I'm the only one who uses a cauldron."

"It's not the cauldron that scares me." His lashes drew down, darkening his eyes. His tone had become chilly. He pointed to my bracelet. "Plus, there was an owl symbol just like the one dangling from your wrist."

I wrapped my hand around the charm. There was something in my gut that told me I was going to Hidden Hall for more than just honing my psychic skills and an intuition class.

"At least you have Mr. Prince Charming and Madame Torres to keep you company." Belle gulped. She stared out the Gathering Grove window, unable to look at me.

"Yeah, thanks for your support." Sarcasm dripped from my lips. I too looked out the window and down the street at what I considered my home.

"Hey, Gerald." I tossed the keys to my green El Camino in the air. "Since you love my green machine so much, would you mind starting her up a couple times while I'm gone?"

"Does that include a couple times around the block?" His eyes were filled with delight, just like the customers who tasted his amazing tea.

"Absolutely." I nodded. "Even a trip to Locust Grove to pick up some of those great cupcakes too, if you like."

I tossed the keys in the air and he caught them, slipping them into his pocket.

"I need to get back to my customers." He waved and was off to help the next in line.

Something was brewing. I felt it deep in my bones. I looked up at my little cottage on the hill that overlooked all of Whispering Falls. There was a dark cloud hovering over it like a bomb was about to drop at any time.

Chapter Four

Four o'clock a.m., the alarm gonged and I smacked the snooze button, rolling over toward Mr. Prince Charming. He didn't bother to lift his head or purr when I touched him. We never get up this early. But, we never went to Intuition School either.

Last night, after Belle and I had our little informative session with Gerald, I went back to A Charming Cure to make sure everything was ready to go. My, the gossip spread.

Most of the village population trickled in and out of shop to get the 411 on why Helena had come to town. According to all of them, Helena never showed up unless there was a big problem. Most of them were happy to hear that I was going to school and maybe be the President of the village when Izzy retires, which made me happy since I had no idea what I was doing.

Use your intuition. Is all that Darla had written in the journal she had left behind? I reached over and turned the alarm off, briefly touching the green leather-bound journal of my mother's last words.

Darla never kept any keepsakes. She said that the memories I needed to keep were the ones in my head.

When my father was murdered, my mother left the village in order to keep me safe and tried to live a normal life. I was little, and slowly a few memories were coming back to me. Somehow she knew I would find my way back to my roots, because she left the journal in the shop. She wrote about her time in Whispering Falls and a few tips of advice for me. Granted it was motherly advice, nothing spiritual or psychic because she wasn't. But, she did let me know who I could and couldn't trust within the village.

The globe next to the journal was completely black. I braced myself for what was going to happen when I tapped it. If four a.m. was too early for me, it was certainly too early for Madame Torres.

"Here goes nothing," I whispered loud enough for Mr. Prince Charming to open one eye.

Tap, tap, tap. Pulling back away from the globe, I raised the sheet over half my face. Nothing happened.

Knock, knock, knock! My knuckles rapped on the glass. A bright orange glow immediately lit up the room.

Madame Torres' red hair was sticking up all over the place. Her eyes darted between mine with the look of death.

"June! It's too early to seek anyone!" My sassy crystal ball yelled back at me.

"Shh!" I pulled the covers over my head. I knew she was going to be mad. "I know I should've told you last night about having to get up early, but I didn't feel like dealing with you when I got home."

Who knew crystal balls could talk? I certainly had never dealt with a crystal ball, much less a snarky one.

"Do you know its four o'clock *in the morning*?" Madame Torres' tried to tame her hair by putting her turban on her head. I tried not to smile at the cock-eyed hat, but it was hard not to. "What? Just because I'm supposed to be at your beck and call, doesn't mean I have to like it."

It was true. Madame Torres' crystal ball was meant for me. The story was that every crystal ball has an owner, but it might take years for them to find each other. I had no clue I was looking for a crystal ball when I stepped foot in Izzy's shop, Mystic Lights, my first day in Whispering Falls.

Madame Torres told me I was in trouble and knew things I didn't even know. According to the law, Madame Torres was my crystal ball and now I'm stuck with the small round glass ball with attitude.

"You'd better get ready." I had no clue how long it took her to get ready. Some days she was all dolled up and other days I'd wake her up from a slumber and I'd never wish my worst enemy to deal with her. "We are starting Intuition School today."

The globe went black.

Tap, tap, tap.

The globe was black with gold stars floating all around.

"Funny, Madame Torres. I know it's night time, but we have to do this." I hated to pull out the big guns, but she left me with no choice. "Did you know that I'm the Dean's niece?"

"Of course I knew, but I wasn't going to tell you." Her voice broke out into a yawn. "That means you can be late to Intuition School. Good night!"

The globe went black again.

I threw back the covers. Mr. Prince Charming still didn't move.

"Were you on the crystal ball clearance table?" I muttered. Who was in charge here? I certainly wasn't.

I grabbed the crystal ball and made my way to the kitchen.

"Whoa!" Madame Torres was wide awake now. Not looking good, but awake. "You know I get sea-sick when you roll me around like that without warning me."

The red light on the coffee pot lit up when I pushed it, letting me know that my hot cup of energy was coming up. The fireflies darting outside my window caught my attention. I didn't have time to tell Eloise, a Fairiwick who lived on the outskirts of Whispering Falls and Darla's best friend, that I was going away to school. I knew the fireflies would let her know.

The fireflies loved to gossip or spy on people. Besides, it was *only* four days. I'm sure no one would even realize I was gone.

"I don't like a back-talking crystal ball. You are going to go to Intuition School whether you like it or not." The coffee smelled good as it percolated. I held the ball up to the window so Madame Torres could see them playing around.

"Ah, to be young again and be able to sleep *all day*." The globe went black.

I chuckled. She was right. The fireflies were the teenagers in the village. Just like the pubescent humans, they roam and play all night and then sleep all day. I set

Madame Torres down by the coffee pot to leave her with the fresh, awakening smell while I jumped in the shower.

With a quick wash and rinse, I hopped out when I heard my cell ringing. Intuition School better not be cancelled or I'm going to be one mad homeopathic cure maker.

"Hello?" I noticed it was Oscar. What in the world was he doing up so early? "Oscar, is everything okay?"

"It sure is." I could hear his smile through the phone. It wasn't unusual for me to wake up in the middle of the night when we were teenagers to find Oscar crawling through my bedroom window. We really thought we were being rebellious, but all we would do is go hide under his big Oak tree and eat Ding Dongs until he was sick. I could eat a million and never get sick.

"I wanted to wish you luck at Intuition School today."

"Listen, I'm doing my time and coming back to live my life." I toweled off and wrapped my robe around me. Even though I gave Helena a hard time about classes, I was a tad-bit excited to find out exactly what I was capable of doing with my "gift". "I will report back and won't leave out any details."

Since I had agreed to do the fast couple of day course, I had to stay on campus and Oscar was going to look after my cottage and shop.

It hadn't been long since I moved here, but the cottage feels more like home than the Cape Cod I owned in Locust Grove. Granted, my parents owned the cottage when they lived in Whispering Falls, so I was sure somewhere deep in my soul the comfort of knowing that was there. It was good to find out that they stilled owned it, just in case I did come back. They were right.

The little family room had all the comforts of home. The natural wood crown-molding accented the vibrant orange fabric on the chairs and couches. There were two bedrooms, of which I only use one. I thought about putting Mr. Prince Charming in one, but he's my fairy god-cat and he needs to be next to me like he has been for the last fifteen years.

"Wake up sleepy head," I called over to the lazy feline. He was going to Intuition School too. There was no way I was going to leave him behind.

Mewwwl, mewl. His mouth gaped open into a wide yawn exposing all his pointy teeth, his back arched with his front paws stretched way out in front of him. He did a couple quick circles and lay by down.

"Don't get too comfortable." The clasp on my charm bracelet took a little longer than normal to clip. I guess my eyes really weren't adjusted to the time. "You are going with me and not leaving my side. And I'm not talking about the bracelet."

I played with my charm bracelet. Bella said Mr. Prince Charming had picked out protective charms. There was no better time like the present to be protected. Going to school made me nervous and uneasy. And my intuition told me stay on alert, even though it was *only* four days.

With suitcase in hand, charm bracelet clasped around my wrist, Mr. Prince Charming by my side, and Madame Torres neatly tucked in my purse along with my Ding Dong, we were off to school. Something I never thought I would do.

The early morning air was brisk. The fog hung just above the tree line as we entered the forest behind my cottage. Using my intuition and Mr. Prince Charming's lead, I knew we were on the right track to Hidden Hall A Spiritual University.

We passed the big rock where all the smudging ceremonies in the village take place. A rock I know very well since I'm the master of ceremonies with my homeopathic skills. As a community, we celebrate everything around the rock.

The last celebration was to welcome all spiritualists to the village. I held a smudging ceremony to clear the way from any negative juju from the past rules. We had a small parade through town and tea at Gathering Grove. Chandra Shango did free pedicures and manicures.

I love the little cauldron she painted on my thumb.

Looking back, I gazed over Whispering Falls through a small clearing. My heart swelled. I had never really felt at home until I moved here.

"Come on," I sighed and coaxed Mr. Prince Charming along, even though I knew we really wanted to be back in bed and then go open the shop for the day. I continued to repeat the motto I was going to adapt while I was gone, "It's only four days. What can happen in four days?"

We came to a sign in the middle of a wheat field. I had never ventured this far out of the Whispering Falls village. The sign had several long wooden arms, each with a finger pointing in a different direction. I set my luggage down next to me and shook my hands out. It was a little heavier than I was use to carrying.

Meow, meow. Mr. Prince Charming planted his butt next to the suitcase.

"Listen, I didn't know what type of shoes I needed to bring." I rolled my eyes. Who in the world needed a testy fairy god-cat? "A girl can never have too many shoes."

"Eye of Newt Crystal Ball School, Tickle Palm School, Intuition School. Oh! Intuition School must be that way."

The problem was, the sign pointed in the direction of a big empty wheat field. And there was no way I was going to walk through that! Especially with my new heels.

I looked down at my new grey jumpsuit. It had been sitting in the closet waiting for the perfect opportunity to be worn. It didn't make me look like a teenager, and it didn't make me look like an old lady. It was perfect; comfortable and cute, especially if I was going to be sitting in the classroom all day long.

But the heels were a different story. I wasn't use to wearing anything other than my flip flops or tennies, but I couldn't resist the little added hot pink color that went well with grey.

"Hmm. . ." I did a 360-degree turnaround, wondering where this Hidden Hall A Spiritualist University was.

Mewl, mewl. Mr. Prince Charming did a complete circle eight, stopped, looked up at the sign, and back at me.

"Do you know where we are supposed to go?" Talking to him like he really did know made me feel stupid, but he was my fairy-god cat, so maybe it wasn't so dumb.

His tail shot up and did a double pump in the air like he was pointing to the sign.

"Yep, it says that way." I tapped the arrow on the sign and, as if magic, a pathway appeared across the wheat field.

My eyes followed as the path gained momentum and ended at a small yellow cottage that had window boxes under each window that overflowed with Geraniums, Morning Glories, Petunias, Moon Flowers, and Trailing Ivy leaving a rainbow of colorful explosion.

The awning flapping in the light breeze read Intuition School in lime green Calligraphy.

"I guess it's time to go to school." I shook my head, grabbed my suitcase, and followed Mr. Prince Charming up the path.

I would have never thought that at twenty-five, I'd been going back to school, especially one for spiritualists.

"You're late." The door swung open before I made it to the top of the step of the schoolhouse. The woman's voice preceded the swift swing of her purple cloak, revealing a much-welcomed face.

"Eloise!" My nerves gave way once I saw Darla's best friend Eloise Sandlewood who just happens to be Oscar's aunt standing at the door.

Her emerald eyes darkened as she picked at the edges of her short, razor-cut hair. "We didn't have time to wait for you." She tapped her watch with her long-red fingernail. "Class started ten minutes ago."

She backed out of the way to let me through.

"I'm sorry." I pointed behind me. "I would've been here on time, but I didn't know you had to touch the sign to. . .uh. . ."

Blankly they all stared at me. There was an entire group of college-aged students with their eyes all on me.

"Huh, some psychic she is." The petite, long blond-haired woman, who looked to be the same age as me, snickered to the other woman sitting next to her.

"I'm sure she'll have privileges. I heard the Dean is her Aunt," the other one whispered back and pulled her long black hair around her shoulder pretending she wasn't talking.

"*She's* the Dean's niece?" the blond bimbo asked as her onyx eyes glared at me before she scribbled something down on a piece of paper, and then slipped it into her bag.

I put my suitcase next to the door, and ran my hands down my new outfit. These girls were definitely more high-fashioned than I was.

Only four days, I repeated over and over in my head. Four days was easy peesy.

The waving arms of a girl sitting in the front row caught my eye. "Over here." Her round face lit up as she patted the stool next to her. She pushed the files and books lying on the table in front of the empty stool.

I smiled and took my place next to her. Mr. Prince Charming jumped on the stool behind me. "Comfortable?" I whispered, looking at him cross-eyed. I swear he smiled back.

"Let's welcome June Heal." Eloise gave a brief introduction to the class of ten." She's just discovered her psychic talents. She lives in the Whispering Falls village. Please be sure to welcome June."

My cheeks deepened to crimson as she bought attention to me. I wanted to crawl under the table and blend in with the floor.

Every one of the girls were very feminine, from their long dark lashes to the very last perfectly pedicure toes. I slid my heels under the stool in hopes they didn't see my manicured toes I had attempted on my own. . .not a great job. But I was proud of my nails that Chandra had done.

"Okay, let's get back to class." Eloise grabbed the mortar and pestle. She ground and mixed the concoction before she added it to the copper cauldron along with a dash of topaz flakes, cobalt globules, and some mandrake root.

The frothy, glowing mixture with the color of gold smelled exactly like nuts and grapes.

"Umm. . ." Collectively the class breathed in the fragrances and continued to write something. Feeling a little left out, I took out a pen and opened my notebook. I doodled a couple of potions I had been working on to help cure my nightmares.

Luckily, I hadn't had one in a few weeks, but I wanted to be prepared just in case they ever came back.

I looked down at the bracelet, touched it and recalled the real Nightmare School.

"June," Eloise brought me out of my thoughts, "would you like to test the new potion?"

Was this a trick question? My eyes narrowed, looking at her suspiciously. "No."

The bubbly girl next to me nudged me, taking me off guard and I fell off the stool.

The class erupted in laughter.

"I'm so sorry." The spunky woman jumped off her stool and ran over to help me out. "But you better volunteer. I'm Hili."

Hili helped me up and I got back on my stool. Mr. Prince Charming hung his head.

Really? Was he ashamed of me? Instantly I wished Mr. Prince Charming were only a cat and *not* my fairy-god cat. I was beginning to miss the days I didn't feel self-conscious around him.

Eloise slid across the floor to my table, and stood directly in front of me. "And why won't you have a little taste?" She smiled, holding the ladle up with the potion bubbling to the top and held it close to my lips.

"Because it will taste bad," I said and fanned my hand in front of my nose.

"You can't smell the juicy grapes?" The snide question came from the blonde. Her hand shot in the air. "I'll taste it, Professor Sandlewood."

Eloise didn't wait for her to ask a second time. She scurried over and dumped the full scoop of potion in the girl's mouth.

The angelic face so fair and lovely contorted and squished up. Her onyx eyes were as big as the night's full moon. Suddenly she jerked and her eyes focused on mine.

"How does rot and spit taste?" I cackled with a smile tickling my soul. I couldn't help it. She deserved that nasty taste and what was about to come next. "Nighty-night." I waved my fingers.

"You are a b. . ." Her eyes rolled back in her head and down she went. Smack dab on the floor, down for the count. Her limbs were sprawled every which way, smoke coming from the stench that oozed out of her pores.

The room fell silent, as every death eye fell on me. Horror showed in their faces.

Slowly I stood up, clapping, and cheering all at once. "Whoo hoo!! What's her name?" I nudged Hili.

She leaned away from me. Even *her* eyes showed fear. "Umm. . .I don't think you should be laughing."

"Why?" I shrugged my shoulders. "She'll be fine. What's her name?"

"Faith," Hili whispered, not looking at me. She leaned back as if she didn't want to associate with me anymore.

Everyone stared with disbelief.

"What?" I circled around the room giving every one of them eye contact. They ducked away from me as if I were some wicked witch. "Eloise gave her a sleeping potion. She'll wake up soon. It smells wonderful, but tastes nasty. Eeck." My tongue darted in and out as if I was trying to get a bad taste out of my own mouth.

"You mean Professor Sandlewood?" The black-haired girl next to Faith didn't seem to worry about her friend as much as she seemed to worry about my relationship with Eloise. "Or are you on a first name basis?" Her eyes glowed with a savage fire.

Hiss, Hiss. Mr. Prince Charming didn't like her tone.

Chapter Five

Eloise. . .er. . . Professor Sandlewood dismissed class early on account of sleeping beauty. According to Eloise. . .er. . .Professor Sandlewood, that was a lesson in itself. You can't judge a potion by the smell. That was why they worked so well. Someone could slip you a potion that tasted like chocolate, but had a death wish inside.

The entire class freaked when she passed out, but what kind of student were they if they didn't use their intuition in Intuition School of all places? The sleeping potion was one of the easiest potions out there. According to the potion book that went along with class.

"June, not everyone is born with the intuition gift like you. You are a natural." Eloise straightened the bottles on her desk. She strained to pick up the copper cauldron.

"They have to have some type of intuition." With both hands on one side, I helped her empty the pot in the sink.

"Just because you are born into a family of psychics or Fairiwicks doesn't mean you have the ability." The sleeping potion slid out of the cauldron and oozed down the drain. She nodded toward sleeping beauty that was still laid flat-out on the floor. "Faith Mortimer is a prime example."

"Is she a Fairiwick or psychic?" Really, there wasn't a whole lot of difference between the two worlds. Fairiwicks were recently welcomed into the Whispering Falls village. They were a product of an interracial relationship between a witch and fairy. Eloise and Oscar were both Fairiwicks. Me, I was a psychic, but for some reason I felt a little magic in my tippy toes. But this was all so new to me. I had no clue as to what my abilities were. I relied on my intuition to guide me.

Just like the sleeping potion. I'd never made it before, but I had skimmed through the class book and most of the ingredients were pretty simple. As I had watched Eloise mix it, my intuition put them together creating an image of a pillow in my head.

Images were powerful to me and when one vividly came to my mind, I paid attention.

"She's a Fairiwick from the East coast." She smiled. There was a wicked glow illuminating from her emerald eyes. She tapped her temple. "She's not very intuitive. That's why she is here."

Eloise cleaned the cauldron. I made it a point to watch. Working with cauldrons was unfamiliar to me, but I had begun working with the one at Charming Cures. They were much faster than the test tubes I had used in Locust Grove.

She used a towel to wipe the remaining ooze and then a dead man's finger to scrape the sides. She sprayed a mist from a bottle that I had never seen.

"Why am I here?" My intuition was my greatest gift that I knew of.

She fanned her hand over the cauldron and with her eyes closed she chanted, "Around the spirits, aura, and dreams, make this cauldron clean for its means."

A thin substance rose with grey oddiments and dissipated into the air.

"Now then," Eloise said as if nothing was going on. She rubbed her hands down her apron. "Let's talk."

She grabbed my suitcase, glanced over at Faith, and wrapped her other hand around my shoulder guiding me out the door. Mr. Prince Charming followed.

"What about her?" I pointed to sleeping beauty.

"The teenagers will watch over her." The day had given over to nightfall and the fireflies had already gathered near the window. "They love to really bother people after they pass out during intuition class."

We walked back down the pathway to the sign. Behind us, the path disappeared with every step we took.

"Hidden Hall A Spiritualist University is top secret. Hence the name. You will find it's more magical than psychic because every psychic has a little bit of magic in them." She looked out into the wheat field that stretched for miles in front of us.

Mr. Prince Charming danced ahead of us. His tail swayed above the wheat as he trotted along until Eloise tapped the sign that read *Hidden Village.*

A small town appeared in the distance. Mr. Prince Charming darted off.

"What is that?" My mouth dropped open. I had no idea why I was surprised. There was just no getting use to the life I had been thrown into. Not that I minded it, but I was eager to learn all about it.

"That's University housing. This is where you will sleep." Eloise continued to walk down the new path she had created. Without a word, I followed her.

The closer we got, the more anticipation grew and deposited a lump in my throat. I recognized a few of the students gathered at Black Magic Café enjoying their mochas until they stopped and stared at us.

"Don't pay any attention to them." Eloise smiled at them and nodded politely, her hands clasped in front of her. They went back to talking among themselves. "They are all curious about the Dean's niece. We didn't know she had any family. Darla never mentioned her to me either."

"So am I," I muttered. I wasn't use to this attention now or ever. We stopped at a gate in front of a small white cottage that was situated across the street from Once Upon a Spell Library.

"That's strange." I pointed to the burst of blue sitting directly overtop the library with the brightest rays of sunshine beaming down on it.

"Oh, it's always sunny in the library." Eloise lifted the latch on the gate and pushed it open. She set my suitcase on the sidewalk. "Home sweet home. This is where you will stay every time you have to come to school."

Mr. Prince Charming was already at the door. Eloise bent down and touched a wilted patch of Gerber Daisies. They sprung back to life along with the rest of the flowers near the same soil.

"Exactly what do you mean by every time?" Nervously I picked at my charm bracelet. From what I understood that coming to school was a one-shot deal and I could go home to Whispering Falls and back to my shop, Charming Cures.

"Even though you are here for only four days, you still have to get continuing education. Especially since you didn't grow up in a mystical village." She gestured for me to walk into the fenced in yard.

Mewl, mewl. Mr. Prince Charming stood up and turned his body to the cottage dorm.

"But. . ." I turned around to protest. Eloise was gone. Vanished into thin air.

"You're here!" Hili yelled from the doorway. Mr. Prince Charming ran into the house. "I can't wait to see your room."

I grabbed my suitcase, closed the gate behind me and walked into my temporary, very temporary, home.

It was much larger than it looked from the outside. Several girls milled around the hallway, walking up and down different staircases and in and out of rooms. A few noticed the new girl. . .me. But didn't pay too much attention.

My heels clomped on the black hardwood floors as Hili's voice rang above everyone else's, "This is June Heal. She's new," she repeated every time we passed someone.

There were a few hi's, but mainly snarls. Just like
every other woman, no one wants to be at school.
Especially a twenty-five-year-old like me.

We took the second set of stairs just off the right of the
entrance and turned right into the long dark hallway. The
lights turned on like falling dominoes. With each step, the
eyes on the women in the framed pictures that lined the
wall shifted, as if they were watching us.

"Don't mind them." Hili shrugged them off. "They are
retired professors making sure we aren't casting any other
spells. Or in your case, psychic ability."

"Casting?" There was a lot I had to learn. I noticed
only three doors in the hallway. Mine, Hili's, and Faith
Mortimer's.

I smacked into the back of Hili when she abruptly
stopped in- between doors. The door to her right had Faith
Mortimer printed on the gold plate and the door to her left
read *June Heal.*

"You're a psychic. I'm completely magic." Pride
swelled on her face. "Cast spells. She twitched her finger in
the air and a spark flew from the tip of it. "This little thing
can be really powerful." She kissed it.

"Voila, this is your room." Hili tapped the name plate. She turned the knob and opened the door. Her eyebrows rose, and her voice escalated, "I've been dying to see it."

There was a piece of paper taped on the door, but Hili ripped it off and held it behind her back.

"What was that?" I tried to glance around her back. She leaned back making me try harder.

"Oh nothing. Just some junk." She waved me off. "Open the door."

"Let me have it." I put my hand out.

She slapped it in my hand.

"UnHidden Hall: The Truth Behind The Magic," I read out loud. "Very catchy and clever."

It was some sort of gossip paper. On the front cover beneath the heading was a picture of me from when I had sold homeopathic cures in the flea market with the heading *Dean's niece? Selling Cures in a Flea Market?*

"Don't read those lies." Hili plucked it out of my hands. "She's just a jealous snob who wished she was the niece of Dean Helena."

Technically, it wasn't a lie. I did sell homeopathic cures out of a flea market booth when I lived in Locust Grove, before I even knew about my spiritualist gift.

"Who puts this out?" I grabbed it back and scanned the article about me coming to the University to learn more about my psychic abilities.

"I really don't know." She shrugged, and then looked around before she leaned in closer. She whispered, "It's put out under a fake name. The rumor is that Faith Mortimer is the editor and she has a few minions that report back all the gossip. I say it's just a whole lot of trash."

I laughed it off. I was only going to be here for four days and I really didn't have anything to hide.

Mr. Prince Charming darted in and out of the room before we could make it in.

Hiss, hiss. That wasn't a good sign. He was good at showing displeasure and he was always right.

I motioned for her to go in the room first. She was way more excited than I was. "I just figured out that I'm her niece, and it's going to take a while for me to get use to having any family, much less being the niece of the Dean of the biggest Spiritual University around."

She smiled, and threw her arms around my neck." I knew we were going to best friends."

I planted a smile on my face, not knowing what to do with that. I was a twenty-five year old woman, not a sorority gal. Little did she know, I wasn't in the market for new friends. I was here to do my time at Intuition School and get back to my life making homeopathic cures in Whispering Falls and Oscar.

I couldn't help but wonder what he was doing.

I pulled away and both of us walked into the room. We stood in awe. Each of us had a different reaction. Hili had a grin as big as the moon on her face, while I flinched and looked away.

"It's amazing. Just like I thought." Hili clasped her hands and twirled in circles.

With her twirls, and all the pink, frilly accessories, the room started to spin. I reached out, grasping the leopard print chair that sat just inside of the massive room that looked as though it had been sprayed with Pepto Bismol all over.

Off to the right was a bathroom, complete with Jacuzzi tub and to the left was a small kitchenette. They had gone through a lot of trouble for me to be here just *four days*.

Pretending to take a closer look at the Jacuzzi tub, I shut the door behind me. Quickly I took Madame Torres out of my bag.

"Let me see Oscar." I rubbed my hands around my crystal ball and concentrated in my mind on his handsome face. I sighed, and then whispered, "Let me see Oscar."

A Charming Cure appeared with Oscar behind the counter with my apron on. A smile crossed my lips. He was talking to a customer and Chandra Shango stood next to him. Her soft hazel eyes zeroed in on the customers' hands as she patted down her short, raspberry colored hair.

My heart skipped a beat. I longed to be there instead of with absent-minded teenager Hili.

Everything looked like it was going well without me. The first day was over and only three more days of school left. What could happen in three days?

I walked out and rolled my eyes when I saw the pink room.

"What's wrong?" Hili tilted her head, looking for any answers to my strange behavior. Granted, most women liked pink, but it was not my color of choice for my living quarters. With a low-whisper, she asked, "Is it too much? It's a fairy's dream."

"A psychic's nightmare," I grumbled back.

She walked over to the bed and grabbed the fluffy pillow and held on to it tight. I walked around taking in all the ruffles, feathers, and *pink.*

"But you are wearing pink shoes." She pointed.

"Yes, but it's a splash of color, not a splatter." *Three days, three days,* I reminded myself.

Hili peeled her hand away from the pillow; she touched the wick of each candle in the chandelier on the bedside table. One-by-one they lit up the room, showing just how much frill there was.

"This room has been waiting for you. And usually the Dean's family comes to school at a very early age." She pulled back and crossed her arms. "Not at twenty-five."

"I've never been a big fan of frill or pink. I won't be here long, so it will be fine." I ran my hand along the satin bedspread. "I'm a jeans and tee kind of gal."

"But you have on heels and a cute jumpsuit!" She stood a little more straight, her posture rigid.

"I wanted to give a good impression for today." I didn't know who I was kidding, but there was no way I was going to dress all fancy, Dean's niece or not. The UnHidden Hall paper was right. I was a girl who grew up in Locust Grove, in a rickety house, with no knowledge of any sort of powers and sold homeopathic cures out of the local flea market.

"Well, we can go shopping at Wands, Potions, and Beyond." Instantly her mood changed. "I do need a new wand for Wand School. They will have all new items."

A sudden knock at the door made us forget about the dreaded room. Before I could answer, Mr. Prince Charming raised up in a full-blown back arch, *hiss, hiss.*

Rapidly, the door flung open, stopping abruptly just shy of the doorstop.

Green smoke danced in the air, and gave way to Aunt Helena. Her black cloak swung open as she stepped into the room, exposing a polkadot A-line skirt and thigh-high pointy red boots that matched her nail color perfectly.

"Wonderful to see you are getting settled in." She waved her hands in the air. Everything pink changed to the oranges and browns that I loved. Instantly, the room became homey and something I would live in. "Now, that should do it. You must forgive the University. Even though we don't know each other all that well, and it's *only three days,* I want you to be comfortable."

"Thank you so much. Hili has been a great help with getting me settled. This will be fine for my four days." I rubbed my temple. I was going to have to watch what I was thinking. Obviously Aunt Helena had been reading my mind.

How did I get here? I wasn't used to all of this. But I constantly needed to remind myself that this was my life now. I was here to learn all of these techniques. I never signed up to be a real psychic or the Dean's niece.

"Hmmm. . ." Helena pierced the distance between them, and then lifted her eyes, glaring at Hili.

Hili rushed out of the room, leaving me alone with Aunt Helena, which made my toes curl. And that was not comfortable in the high-heel shoes. The door automatically closed behind her and then locked.

"How is everything going?" She tried to be sincere, but I just didn't trust her like I did Eloise.

"Fine." I lied.

Eloise would've been a much better Dean. She was so much easier to relate to. After all, Eloise was Darla's best friend and a great help to Darla. Now, years later, she was helping me, even going as far as clearing my name from murder the first week I had moved to Whispering Falls.

Where was Aunt Helena when I did need her? Biting my lip, I looked away in fear she did know what I was thinking. She seemed to have a lot of different powers than a pure psychic, which made me wonder if I was only psychic or did have a touch of Fairiwick in me.

"Dean! Dean!" The other minion that sat next to Faith ran into *my* room. Her eyes darted back and forth between Aunt Helena and me. She jabbed her finger in my direction. Her eyes narrowed on me, casting a shadow in the room. "Come quick! Faith is on her deathbed! No thanks to *her,*" she said, pointing at me.

Chapter Six

"Me? What did I do?" This girl was as crazy as her friend.

"Now, now, Raven." Aunt Helena took her in her arms and comforted her. Suspicion settled in my gut. My intuition told me something was off. Why was Aunt Helena so willing to hug Raven when she had never even *touched* me? And I was supposed to be flesh and blood. "I'm sure Faith is going to be okay."

Aunt Helena rushed us out the door and across the street to the University Infirmary. When we got to Faith's room on the third floor, Eloise was sitting on the bench outside of her door. Her head in her hands, her shoulders bouncing up and down with each sob that came from deep from within her soul.

"Dean Helena, I have no idea what happened." Eloise stood up, her face blotted red. "It was the same sleeping potion we use in 'Don't Judge a Potion by the Smell' class."

Helena didn't answer. She swept her cloak over her body and raised a finger toward Eloise. A spark of blue light shot from her fingertip and hit Eloise, causing Eloise to crumble to the floor in a little ball.

"Stop!" I screamed, crouching to Eloise's side. Out of the corner of my eye, I saw Helena raise her hand again. I threw my hand up in the air. "You are hurting her."

"They need to respect the rules. You are not one of them!" Helena screamed, "You are not a Fairiwick!" Her words were as sharp as her magic. "Professor Sandlewood, you are on administrative leave until further notice."

With a flick of her hand, Helena made Eloise disappear from my arms.

"Where did she go?" I screamed and jumped up, standing nose to nose with an Aunt that loved me no more than she loved the Fairiwicks.

"June, it's a rule. A rule is a rule, and until we figure out what was in the sleeping potion," she brushed her hands down the sleeves of her cloak as if she was wiping away the filth, "it's no secret that Faith is not Professor Sandlewood's favorite student."

What did she mean by that? I didn't see Eloise treat Faith any different than she did the others in the class, but it happened in the first few hours of a very long four days.

Hmmm. . .only four days. What can happen in four days? I thought about my mantra. Evidently, a lot can happen in a few hours.

She disappeared into Faith's room. I looked in the window where Helena stood at the edge of Faith's bed. I opened my bag and grabbed a Ding Dong. If ever there was a situation where I needed a Ding Dong, this was it.

I bit down, relieving a little stress from the chocolaty goodness and sank down on the bench. I wasn't sure what I needed to do. There was no way I was going to let Eloise take the blame for something my gut told me she didn't do.

"Is that good?" Raven stood behind me. The heat from her breath made the hairs on my neck stand up. I turned to face her, and winced when I felt her fingernail jab my arm. "You will regret laughing at Faith in class. Stay away from her."

Oh, I was definitely going to visit Faith Mortimer, but when no one else was around. One way or another I was going to find out who was trying to frame Eloise. . .on the down-low. And I only had a few days to do it in.

Without a word, I watched Raven walk down the hall and around the corner. There was something different about that girl. But I didn't know what. It wasn't like my intuition told me to watch out, but my mind told me to keep a close eye on her. Maybe it was my earlier run-in with her, and now this one that puts my protection instincts on high alert. Especially since she sort of threatened me to stay away.

The faint amber glow coming from the small rectangular window caught my eye. Helena had her arms outstretched over Faith's bed. The yellow light circled Faith, lifting her off the bed just a tad. Helena was chanting something, but I was not a lip reader.

If Helena is my aunt, and we are psychics, how could she do magic? Hmm. . .

I decided not to stay around. My intuition told me something was going on. . .almost evil. I needed Madame Torres' advice on where to go from here.

On the way back, the students were still gathered in the streets, talking about Eloise and the potion she gave Faith. There were even a few shared whispers and pointing in my direction. It seems as if they had already connected the dots between Eloise and me and thought I was just as guilty as she was.

Wands, Potions, and Beyond was still open as I passed it on my way back to my room. If there was one thing I knew I could do, it was make cures. And that was something Faith was in desperate need of.

If I could reverse the potion she drank, or even reverse the spell that someone had bestowed upon her, then I could prove Eloise's innocence.

Entering the store was easy, but trying to find what I needed was a different story. The aisles were labeled with everything that a Fairiwick, Dark-Sider, witch or sorcerer would need, making me a wee-bit envious of all the cool items. Yes, I was turning out to be a magic wannabe. But I was only good at one thing and one thing only….potion cures.

Aisle eight was where they kept the cauldrons. I knew I couldn't get a big one, so the little desktop one would have to do.

The aisle over from the cauldrons had the ingredients I was going to need to start off with. I ran my finger up and down the aisle until my intuition told me to pick a few of the rarer spices. I hoped I was channeling Faith somehow, but deep down I knew I was going to have to stand over her in order to get a real reading on what her body needed to recover. And that was going to have to wait until the

University police and Aunt Helena completed their assessment of her.

Loaded with my armful of goodies, the cashier told me that the items in the store were free to the Dean's family members. So taking advantage of my new title as niece, I accepted it. I was eager to get back and start the cure. After all, not only did Faith rely on it, Eloise did too.

Chapter Seven

After getting back into my room, I took Madame Torres out of my bag while Mr. Prince Charming stood at my feet watching every move I made.

Twisting the cauldron up at all angles, I tried to figure out if it had a switch since it was geared toward the newbie potion makers, but of course, it didn't. Since it was small, I would use it like my big one at home, with much less ingredients.

I grabbed a tissue off my desk to wipe it out, which reminded me to nab the cauldron cleaner from Eloise's classroom. Having something that worked would really be nice.

Taking each spice out of the bag, I lined them up alphabetically.

Meow, meow. I swore Mr. Prince Charming was mocking me.

"You can never be too careful with these potions." I wagged my finger at him. "See what happened to Faith."

He paid me no attention. He jumped up on the bed, finding his way to my pillow, and kneaded it a few times before he finally lay down and curled up.

"Allspice, cinnamon, mandrake, rattlesnake's rattle, and sage." I tapped each one, hoping to get some intuition on what to put in first. Nothing was coming which meant that there was something missing, but what?

I tapped my temple and really concentrated on Faith. There was no way I was getting anywhere near her to figure out what I needed. This was so much easier at Charming Cure when I could physically talk to the person. The only interaction between Faith and I had been our first meeting, and that didn't turn out too well.

All I could picture was her greedy little prissy self, grabbing the ladle full of sleeping potion from Eloise and downing it like a shot.

"Seriously?"

I spun around and clenched my chest. The voice had me jumping out of my own skin.

"Hahahhaa!" Madame Torres cackled as she glowed a brilliant pink. She pointed her long red fingernail at me and threw her head back. "I scared you!"

My stomach clenched and my eyes narrowed. My own crystal ball mocked me.

"You don't appear when I want you to appear." I pointed back. "You appear when *you* want to appear. Those days are over!"

I stomped around the room trying to ignore the little snide remarks she was making under her breath. There was an ingredient I was missing and I had to figure out what it was, not fight with my crystal ball.

"Is that right?"

"Yeah, that's right." I turned back to the cauldron and grabbed the allspice. Opening the lid, I shook a couple dashes into the pot.

"Fine. I was going to tell you that you are missing the main ingredient." Her voice was snippy. "The one ingredient that has been shoved back in the back of your brain."

Was she baiting me? I thought, glaring at her. I couldn't help but wonder why she had picked me to own her. Did she only want someone that she could make fun of?

Who was the psychic here? I waved my hand, ignoring her. But that was impossible. Time was of the essence.

"Ugh!" I turned toward her and planted my balled up fists on my hip. "Fine. What is it?"

"So *now* you want me help?" Madame Torres spoke slowly, throwing her words like stones.

"You know what, you better tell me now before I take you to the Locust Grove flea market when we get home." I threatened. "You are my crystal ball. I tell you when to work. I tell you when I want to see something. You don't go around deciding. I will sell you at that flea market and the buyer will never know what you really are. I will silence you forever."

"You wouldn't?" Her cheeks sucked in at the near mention of going to a flea market.

"Try me." I went nose to glass with her. "Now tell me the ingredient. Eloise and Faith depend on this."

"You need something personal from the recipient. Just like you see them in person in Whispering Falls and know exactly what they need. Only Faith is in a coma." The globe went black. Madame Torres' feelings were hurt and she was only going to give me what I asked for.

Something personal. I racked my brain. *Something personal?* What was more personal than something from Faith's room?

The cauldron circulated and mixed on its own and wasn't doing anything important, so going next door to Faith's room shouldn't be that hard.

The halls were empty when I opened my door, but I tippy- toed anyway. The police tape was crisscrossed across Faith's door to hinder visitors.

Taking no chances, I used the edge of my shirt to turn the knob. I had seen in too many movies how they can trace fingerprints, and that was the last thing that I needed. I might only be a potion psychic, but I knew for sure that 'breaking and entering', and 'tampering with evidence' charges were not in my future.

I looked to my left and right to make sure the coast was clear before I went in, because clearly, the police did not want anyone in there. I went in anyway, and quietly shut the door behind me…using the hem of my shirt.

For a moment, my 'magic wannabe' syndrome kicked in. I really wished I had Hili's gift of touch to light the candles, and since I didn't, I was going to have to feel my way around for a switch.

The room was filled with earth-tone colors, which sent me into a bit of a shock. Faith was not the muted type at all.

Her laptop sat on the desk as if she was just using it, and her room was neatly waiting for her to come back.

Wait! I thought there were no electronics. Besides, wasn't the computer the first item the police takes? I eyed the pink laptop, taking it under my arm in a weak moment of knowing that I needed to learn all about Faith in order to figure out who would harm her and why.

The bed was neatly made and sat underneath the two large windows that faced the front of the house. She had a wall of photos that I quickly glanced through but none of them seemed unusual. A picture of what I assumed were her parents and siblings hung in the middle. Faith was front and center in the shot, smiling ear-to-ear next to a dark haired girl with pigtails. They looked to be about the same age, which made me wonder where her sister was.

The parents appeared to be prim and proper. The gentleman, dressed in a suit, looked to be about six foot tall with neatly slicked hair to one side. The woman had a modest calf-length red dress that hit at her calf and low-heeled shoes. They all seemed to be celebrating something special. Maybe even a magical achievement. Faith was holding up a small wand.

It reminded me of something a mortal family would have, like a first communion or preschool graduation. She was quite cute really, the cutest of the two.

Glancing around, there didn't seem to be anything out of place. It looked like she was a typical college student. Some items hung on the wall that boosted the Hidden Hall extra-curricular activities. There wasn't any sign of a newspaper being secretly produced, but that didn't mean that it wasn't happening somewhere else in Whispering Falls.

The manicure set neatly tucked on the edge of her desk nudged my intuition. . .DNA. Sure, I could use hair from her brush, but something with her fingernails would be the perfect ingredient. Or at least that was what my intuition told me.

Careful not to damage the DNA ingredient, I didn't touch it. My eyes followed the fingernail file dust to the edge of the desk, and then down to the wastebasket.

No, June. You wouldn't. My subconscious mind told me I was a sicko, but I did it anyway. After all, it was for the sake of Eloise. She would've done it to save Darla or me.

I reached into the garbage and took the liner with Faith's fingernail clippings resting on the top. With the laptop and garbage bag in hand, it was time to get out of there.

Once safely back in my room, I pulled a chair up to the wall and unscrewed the air conditioning vent. Faith's laptop fit nicely into the hole and no one would find it if they came looking for it.

My intuition told me there was some important information on there, but first things first. If I could find a cure, now was the time.

"Well, well." Madame Torres decided to make another appearance. There was laughter in her eyes. "I see that you took my advice."

"Flea market!" I yelled over my shoulder as I replaced the screws and went to work with my tweezers in the garbage bag.

Purrr, purr. Mr. Prince Charming didn't even lift his head off my pillow.

The cauldron had begun to boil which was a sure sign that all the ingredients had been aligned.

One-by-one I used the tweezers to drop Faith's fingernails into the pot.

Swoosh! The cauldron glowed with a shiny potion that turned yellow with orange streaks running through it like lightning flashes.

I stepped back in case a few sparks flew with the other ingredients at the ready. After a few more dashes of this and that, the cauldron shut off, letting me know that the potion was complete.

With my nose in the air, I took in a deep breath, hoping to catch a hint of a scent. The potion was intended for Faith and knowing what she really liked would've helped. But there was nothing out of the ordinary. I chalked it up to her current state of the coma. She wasn't probably in any shape to like anything at the moment.

Dang. I sat on the edge of the bed feeling a little elated that I might have a cure, but a little defeated in the fact that there was no smell. This wasn't a guarantee, but definitely worth a shot.

I reached over and pulled my purse closer. I didn't have to dig too far to grab a Ding Dong. Having a little treat might jog my insight on what I needed to do. When I bit into the yummy goodness, I realized I didn't have anything but my empty coffee cup to put the potion in. Like magic, the treat was gone in a couple of bites.

It was time to test my real skill and get the potion for the intended recipient. . .Faith.

Chapter Eight

The framed retired professors hanging on the wall seemed to never sleep. They watched my every step as Mr. Prince Charming and I darted down the stairs and out into the empty street.

It was late, and hopefully no one would be around to see me or to tattle on me to Aunt Helena. She was the last person I wanted to find out that I was making a cure, let alone one for Faith. Especially when the rules clearly stated that you couldn't make potions on your own, or at least on University property.

We slipped into the hospital and into Faith's room unseen. Faith remained in the same position since I last saw her. The tubes connected to her made the machines beep at a steady pace.

Looking at her, I'd sworn she was a goner. Dark circles under her eyes made her pale skin appear as if she had two big black eyes. Her ashen skin was no longer the gothic pale that made her features stand out even more, making her the exotic looking creature that she was.

Even her fingernails had grayed.

Mewl, mewl. Mr. Prince Charming jumped up on her bed. He was as uncomfortable as I was.

"Sicko, I know." I hated to admit that this was not my finest hour. I ran my fingers from the bag of the IV to where it entered into her hand and wondered how in the world I was going to get the potion into the little tube.

If only. . .my magic wannabe struck again. I wished I could just wave a magic wand and bring her back. Unfortunately, magic didn't work that way. At least mine didn't.

"Potion maker, not doctor." I whispered, reminding myself that this concoction probably wasn't going to work.

There was no way I was going to inject something in her, so I stood over her lifeless body and parted her lips with one hand. With the other, I tipped the used coffee cup that was filled with the potion, into the opening of her mouth. The thick liquid fell in one big drip.

A zap went through my hand. An electric shock traveled through my body, propelling me against the wall, and then down to the floor. Mr. Prince Charming landed next to me.

Hiss, Hiss. Mr. Prince Charming batted at the door. The light underneath the door gave way to shadows of someone's shoes.

"Some fairy-god cat you are. Come on." I crawled to Faith's bed, and then rolled under. I couldn't risk someone seeing us. Mr. Prince Charming ran under too.

The door flung open, the lights flipped on, and two nurses rushed in. One punched buttons on the machine that was beeping much faster than it had been when I first got there, and the other did some sort of diagnostic test on Faith.

Please don't let me have done her in, I thought with my eyes shut tight and hands clasped in praying position. All sorts of thoughts began to flood in.

What if I wasn't a real psychic? What if I just fed her a deadly concoction? What if Eloise really did do it? What if my intuition really isn't that great?

"She still has a pulse." One of them said.

"This is the strangest thing. Her fingernails. Look." The other's voice raised an octave.

There was a collective gasp between the two. The only thing we could see was the shuffling of their feet as they went around the bed.

"We need to get the doctor." Their white nursing shoes proceeded to run out of Faith's room.

"Let's go." I rolled out from under the gurney bed and Mr. Prince Charming followed.

The nurses left the lights on. My body froze in place. I stared at Faith. Speechless.

Mewl, mewwl.

"I'm coming." I waved him off as I bent down to get a better look at the glowing hot pink nails. It looked as if Faith had just step out of A Cleansing Spa back in Whispering Falls.

My eyes slide up her body and to her face. She still had the grayness and the black eyed looked, but the nails. . .All my what if's had flown right out the door.

Chapter Nine

We ran back to the cottage dorm before the nurses came back to Faith's room with the doctor. It was late and it had been a long day. I was tired, but the cure was more alive than ever. I was going to have to wait until morning to see if anything other than her fingernails coming back to life had transpired from the concoction.

If I didn't get some sleep, I'd never make it to Intuition class. Now it was more important than ever to be on time and fit in with the other students.

The more I tried to close my eyes, the more my eyes refused to close. Haunting images of Eloise in some Hidden Hall prison cell corrupted my mind along with the unknown potion I had given Faith.

"You know you can see her." Madam Torres made her first appearance since our arrival and since her little tantrum on our way here.

"Nice to see you." I sat on the edge of my bed. A smile formed across my face. "And you fixed your hair. And I love the color choices." I referred to her long, curly red mane that took up most of the glass globe. The green glow illuminated the ball, which made her red lips stand out on her purple face.

"Well." She shook her loose curls. "I've heard all about these college men." She rubbed her lips together, making them a darker shade of crimson.

Mewl, mewl. Mr. Prince Charming let us know he was there. He made three circles and plopped down. He was having no problem sleeping.

"I'm not surprised you aren't sleeping. Especially after the potion you just gave Faith." Her left eyebrow cocked up in true Elvis Fashion. "I hope you brought some concealer for those under-eye circles."

If she thought she was being funny. . .she wasn't.

"After all, the Dean's niece can't be looking. . .umm . . .nearly dead. Plus I can't be looking bad because of you." She flung her hair to the back of the globe. The water swooshed to the front.

"Whatever. I still don't get why it's such a big deal that I'm related to that woman." I had no time to play pretty, pretty dress up. I had to find Eloise. "Let's get back to what you were saying about me seeing Eloise."

I had done all I could do for Faith, at least until I see
how the potion affected her. I did need a plan to help
Eloise, but what?

"Hmm. . ." Madame Torres disappeared. The green
globe went from opal to orange, and then brown. The drab
color floated to the bottom and cleared the globe. "Your
wish."

I heard Madame Torres, but didn't see her. The ball
showed a picture of Eloise hunkered down on a dirt floor
with a chain around her ankle that was shackled to the
concrete wall. She was being treated like a cruel animal.
That was definitely one thing that needed to be
changed…the way they treated their prisoners.

Eloise had already been through so much. For twenty-
years she had been banned from Whispering Falls and lived
a life of solidarity. All because she was a Fairiwick. She
didn't deserve this.

"Eloise," my hush voice dripped with sadness. Tears
flooded my eyes seeing her in that position. I didn't realize
I could see anywhere I wanted. I was under the impression
I could only see the places I owned, like A Charming Cure
and my home.

As if she could hear me, she looked up. Her alabaster skin was even gaunter. Almost ghost-like.

"Help me," her lips mouthed. The ball went black.

"Where is she?" I pleaded with Madame Torres. The globe remained black.

"I have no idea. That is something you have to find out."

"Thank you." I grabbed Madame Torres off her pedestal on the night stand and kissed all over the glass. I was glad that she showed me Eloise, even if she couldn't give me her location. I was on a mission to find her.

"Pweft, pweft." Madame Torres appeared, and spit specks of silver out of her mouth. "Listen, I'm your crystal ball. A cranky one. I didn't sign up to be a kissing ball." The water cleared and it went back to black. "This is a professional relationship."

"Naw. This is a great friendship." I hugged her and held her tight.

"I'm only here to guide you. Not give you answers." Her voice echoed creating waves in the ball. Like a light switch that had turned off, so had Madame Torres.

The clock read two a.m. and I didn't have to be at Intuition School until seven. Seeing Eloise and knowing she was okay put me at ease. I had a couple of hours to snoop around this University.

Who needs sleep?

I threw on my black jump suit and tennies before I grabbed Madame Torres and threw her in my bag. I could hear a slight tantrum at the bottom of my purse. I was going to ignore her. After al,l she *was* there to help me.

I backed out of my door, and used the key to lock it.

"Where are you going at this hour?"

My heart nearly leapt out of my chest until I realized it was Hili standing in the shadow of the hallway.

"Shh." I put my finger up to my mouth. I didn't want to wake the retired professors on the wall, but it was too late. All of the eyes popped open and darted between Hili and me.

"Why are you all dressed? Where are you going?" Hili had her short, tomboy blonde hair matted to her head in a Michelle Williams kind-of-way, rolled up tight blue jeans, black V-neck tee, and black high-heeled shoes.

"I don't sleep." She shrugged her shoulders. "Where are you off to?" She followed me down the hall, clicking as if she was a little girl playing dress up in her mom's shoes.

I wasn't going to tell her anything with the professors staring.

Walking down the stairs, I reached in my bag and grabbed two Ding Dongs. It was obvious to me and Mr. Prince Charming that Hili was going to tag along.

"Come on." I handed her one of the scrumptious treats wrapped in foil and headed out into the dark night.

The fireflies darted around us. Being nosey teenagers, no doubt. I ignored them and Hili's endless stream of questions.

I really didn't know where I was going. I was relying on my number one gift. My intuition.

"Okay, Hili, how long have you been a student at Hidden Hall." My intuition told me to go the opposite direction of the field to get to Intuition School, so I set my sights on the darker side of the University.

Briefly stopping, I noticed it was also the more dreary side as well.

"Four years." Hili put her hand on me. We stopped.

"Four years? But you are only eighteen." I couldn't imagine leaving home as a young teenager.

"It's different for us." She shrugged it off. "You were raised by a mortal, but if you had two psychic parents, then you would've been here too. Where are you going?"

"This way." I took a few more steps when I realized she wasn't following me. I turned around. "Well, are you coming?"

She'd better be. I'll be damned if I wasted a good Ding Dong on her.

She ducked when a bat aimed at her head, teeter-tottering on her high heels, and then started to plummet to the ground, only to catch her fall. "I don't think that is a good idea. That is where the darker side students live and the professor dorms."

Professor dorms? Darker side?

"What do you mean by darker side?" This was something altogether new to me.

"Well, you have the dark spiritualists that you things like voodoo and dolls. And then you have us. The Good-Siders." She looked into the dark abyss in front of us.

"Are all Dark-Siders bad?" That didn't seem right, but Hili had been a spiritualist all her life so she should know. And it was good to know that there was a term for people like me. A Good-Sider.

"Every once in a while there is a good one in the Dark-Sider group, but not here." She pointed in the direction she didn't want us to go. "I'm not going in."

Dark or not, I am." I turned and looked into the dark before me. I wasn't going to freely admit it, but I was scared out of my wits, and secretly prayed Hili would follow even though I had no idea how she would help if some Dark-Sider did hurt us. Maybe she could use her high-heeled fancy shoes to stab one or even claw their eyes with her perfectly manicured fingernails.

Somehow I doubted that. She didn't seem the type to even go *near* confrontation or dark anything. She was harmless and a little nosy, but it would be great to have some type of backup.

Before ascending into the darkness, I closed my eyes and took in a deep breath. Not just any old inhale, but one that filled my lungs. The kind that gives you the little extra brain oxygen to give you courage. Only my brain was telling me I was crazy.

Forcing myself, I took the first step into the dark and opened my eyes. The only thing I could see was Mr. Prince Charming's tail dancing along the path in front of me and I could hear Hili's heels clicking behind me.

"Oh…..wait up!" She whispered so loud, I was sure she would wake the owls. Even if she did wake the nighttime creatures, I was relieved she decided to come. Darla always told me that she believed there was strength in numbers.

"What is the layout of the buildings?" I whispered forging ahead and not looking back.

"I have no idea." Hili's teeth chattered with every click of her heels. "I've never been brave enough to come back here."

I glanced over in the direction of her voice, and her brilliant white teeth were shining like white shoe laces do at the skating rink when they turn the strobe on.

"Look." I pointed to a faint light in the distance. One more step and we made it into a clearing where the moon and stars lit up the night sky.

"Wow!" Hili mouth formed an O as her eyes almost popped out of her head.

It was a complete village of tree houses, just like Eloise's house in Whispering Falls. Some were two-stories, while others were three. The trees were connected with wooden bridges, the kind that I would've loved to have had as a child.

"The Dark-Siders don't live so badly." I walked toward the only one with a light on. "I thought you said they stayed up all night?"

"I'm only repeating what I heard." There was a snide tone in her words. "Where are you going?"

I stopped at the bottom step of the tree house and looked up. Someone's shadow danced along the bark of the tree at the top level.

"I'm going up." I put my foot on the first step to see if it was going to make noise.

"Are you crazy?" Fear, stark and vivid, glittered in her eyes. "June Heal, I think you are crazy. I'm staying right here." She stomped and her heels sank in the ground. She tugged, and tugged a little more, but one of her shoes wouldn't come out.

"While you work on that," I pointed to her foot, "I'm going to see who's up there."

As she continued to pull and groan, I followed Mr. Prince Charming up the steps around the bark of the tree toward the light.

Once at the top, I briefly stopped and looked around. Who ever lived here had the most amazing view. I felt like I could almost grab a star and put it in my pocket for keeps.

Oscar would love this; I thought and smiled wondering how he was doing with the shop. The sudden movement of a shadow that was cast on the trunk of the tree caught my attention and I bent down into the shadow.

I tucked my hair behind my ear and leaned over, looking into the window to see if I recognized the Dark-Sider. The long onyx hair and pale skin told me exactly who it was.

Raven.

I stood as still as the night as I watched her glide around the large room. She reached in a cabinet and pulled out a cauldron. She hung it on the hook in the fireplace and touched it. A spark shot out from the underneath the cauldron and a flame ignited, causing the liquid in the cauldron to quickly boil over.

Was she making a dark potion?

I didn't know anything about dark potions, but I was on a mission to find out everything I could. I had a sneaky suspicion that Raven was now a big part of Faith Mortimer's fate as well as Eloise's. If Raven was such a good friend to Faith, and she knew a lot about potions, why hadn't she stopped Faith from drinking the sleeping potion?

A bright red plume of smoke cast a shadow over the large room. It dangled over the two large, black leather sofas and coffee table. The smoke extended from the fireplace mantle to the hallway leading to other rooms I couldn't see.

"Oh, no." I gasped, realizing a shiver of panic as the red plume developed into a skull and crossbones. The mouth of the skull opened and closed as if it was laughing at me. Sheer black fright swept through me, remembering what Gerald had said about the skull and crossbones. I continued to watch Raven perform her dark magic.

Carefully she took different ingredients from a makeshift box. These weren't packaged like my cures. These were different.

I strained to see what she picked first. Unscrewing the lid off the bottle, she pinched out a small portion of Cimicifuga, which didn't phase the potion with a spark or color. I made mental notes to remember what each of these ingredients was so I could look them up in the Magical Cures book.

She shook a bottle labeled Nuxvomica, sending a couple dashes into the mix. That caused a couple of sparks that hit the red plume above and popped it like a needle popping a balloon.

Suddenly the air smelled like pinecones. As soon as she used the Apis ingredients, the air smelled like pine needles.

Who likes pinecones, pine needles or anything outside? Raven was making a cure with someone in mind and I was going to find out who.

My eyes drifted to the mantel as Raven chanted something. I couldn't make out the words.

I squinted, trying to see who she had in the frames. Two little girls. One black haired, one blonde.

Faith. Quickly I closed my mouth, fearing I was going to make a noise. Mr. Prince Charming looked back and darted down the steps. It was my cue to go, but I had to get a closer look at those photos. Had they been friends all of their lives? But how? One was a Dark-Sider, while the other was a Good-Sider.

Slowly I crept up to the window and peered in. Raven's eyes were closed as her hands whipped over the cauldron so fast that I couldn't even follow them. The pot boiled and bubbled creating a mess in the fireplace, but

Raven didn't seem to notice. She was completely in a dark zone.

A green stream of light passed over my right shoulder from the house. Glancing at the window to see where it came from, Raven stood, stoned faced, red cheeks, glowing green eyes. She knew I was there.

I darted down the stairs, past Hili, and out of the woods.

Chapter Ten

We didn't talk about what had just happened, what I saw, or even her shoe. We walked in silence trying to figure one another out.

We made it back without being seen or what I considered not being seen even though the retired professors that hung on the wall watched our every move up the stairs.

"There was a framed picture on the mantle of Faith and Raven from when they were little. I mean toddler-little. I find it odd that they have been best friends for. . .ever." I shuffled my foot along the floor while I looked down, noticing that Hili only had one shoe on.

"Where is your shoe?" My mouth dropped.

"I couldn't get it out of the mud. And you took off so fast that I left it there." Her words were rushed and panicked.

"Oh, Hili." I smacked my forehead with the palm of my hand. "Now they are going to know that we were there."

"I've never been into the woods until now. I didn't know it was so muddy. Come on." She waved me toward her room. "I have a coffee pot my dad sent me. I'll make us a cup before we have to go to class."

"If anyone asks, just say that I was curious about the University and you decided to go with me. Nothing more." I crisscrossed my fingers over my heart. "Promise?"

She crisscrossed. "Promise."

Her room was everything I never wanted in my room. The leopard print was plastered everywhere including the rug and wall hangings. Pictures of a happy family displayed all over the walls showed Hili smiling in each of them. Hili was one pampered daddy's girl.

"That's my daddy." She smiled, proud as could be. "He wants me to be really successful in school. How do you know Professor Sandlewood?"

"She and my mother were best friends." I continued to pick up little knick-knacks she had sitting around her room. "She helped me get through a really hard time when I first moved to Whispering Falls"

"Do you think she really hurt Faith?" She asked. She walked over to the mirror she had hanging on the wall and corrected the lining of her lipstick. "I mean, she *really* didn't like Faith."

"I know she didn't hurt Faith." The coffee smelled really good. "How do you know they didn't get along?"

"You know. Teacher student stuff." She waved her hands in the air. A little spark left her pointer finger. She giggled. "Sorry. Sometimes it goes off without me making it. That's why I go to school."

"Can't you give me a specific?" I wasn't a 'just-cause-you-should-know' kind of girl. I wanted pure, hard, facts as to why Faith and Eloise had a strained relationship.

"Faith is so uppity and thinks that she should pass because of her family money. Professor Sandlewood makes you work." Hili took two mugs from the closet. I peeked in, but she slammed it shut before I could see anything.

Curiosity had gotten the best of me. "What's in here?" I put my hand on the door knob, ready to twist it.

"Please don't go in there." She blushed. "It's my closet. I'd be so embarrassed for you to see how messy it is."

I could just imagine what all she had in there. Hili was one high-maintenance teenager. . .harmless none the less.

"Do you get along with Faith?" It wasn't a bad question to ask. They both seemed to come from high-class Good-Sider's.

"We've never had a problem. She has her friends and I have mine." She poured the coffee out of the carafe. The steam from the heat rolled up and formed a heart before it puffed out. She handed me my cup. "My dad is so cute. He had the coffee pot specially made to do that."

Yes, she was just as high-class as Faith Mortimer.

"Sometimes we get accelerated students like you." She sat down. "Most the time they are just here to hone their abilities."

"What about the professors?" I questioned. Eloise didn't even mention she was a professor, nor did Izzy tell me.

"They come from all over. There are Dark-Siders along with the Good-Siders like us." She got up and took a couple mugs that were in the shape of a witch's hat. "Cream? Sugar?"

A Ding Dong sure would taste good right now, I thought as I sat down to drink my coffee. Only I wasn't into sharing anymore. I only had a few left as it was. Because it was only four days. . .*right?*

"Where are the professor offices?" Somehow I had to get to the student files and read Raven's and Faith's.

Maybe their background would lead me in a direction to help Eloise.

"It's on the backside of the library. Why do you ask?" She tilted her head to the side.

"I thought I'd pay my aunt a visit." I lied. "We have a lot of catching up to do."

Yes, a Ding Dong would taste great right now.

I glanced over, noticing Hili's clock read 7AM in hot pink glow numbers.

"We are late!" I jumped up and out the door before I even thought about grabbing my bag or Madame Torres, leaving them on Hili's bed.

I ran out of the cottage dorm and down the street quickly touching the sign that pointed in the direction of Intuition class.

That didn't stop me from thinking about Elosie. Things didn't add up. There was no way she'd hurt Faith. Plus Darla would never put me in danger. At least that's what my intuition told me.

Chapter Eleven

"Glad to see you made it." Helena glared at me with a burning, reproachful eye.

I took a seat next to Hili, wondering how in the hell she got there faster than me. And then I realized that she must've cast herself there. What a friend she was. She should've cast me right alongside of her.

The heel that she had lost at the bottom of Raven's house was propped on top of our desk. *Damn, Raven told Aunt Helena we were there.*

Hili slipped the shoe in her bag as she pulled out her books. My embarrassment turned into raw fury as I realized Hili didn't have my back. *She could've reminded me to get my books*, I thought as I glared over at her.

She shrugged her shoulders, and then flipped to the page.

I turned my attention to Helena who was drumming her fingers on the edge of a new cauldron, continuing to stare at our table.

New cauldron? I couldn't help but wonder what happened to Eloise's. It was definitely worth looking into. But why?

Sarsaparilla, Zicum, Rhus Tox, Ledum, Eupbrasia, Ferrum Phos, Belladonna, Mandrak. I read through the potions that lined the shelf behind Aunt Helena. I recognized a few from the Magical Cures book. There was nothing there that Raven had used and I had to be sure to look up the ones she did make. Not to mention try to figure out who likes pinecones. Raven was definitely making a potion for a particular someone. But who?

"Ma'am, June and I. . .um. . ." Hili was about to erupt like a volcano.

"We were taking a walk and I wanted to know my way around the University." My voice escalated, "What's wrong with that?"

Wasn't that a valid question? Why did they want to keep the Dark-Siders and Good-Siders away from each other? I spun around my stool and came face to face with Raven. There was fire in her eyes.

I had no idea if I was right, but Helena didn't protest and I didn't let my lack of confidence break.

My eyes narrowed, and a huge smug, smile crossed my lips. Even Raven couldn't vocally protest, but she discreetly slid her hand across the table and down to Faith's empty seat, patting it as if she was warning me.

Before turning around, I gave her the ole "I'm watching you" fingers like I saw on the movie *Meet The Parents.*

Hili was someone I couldn't rely on. She was young and didn't want to get in trouble, so she would probably tell on me in a minute. I was going to be really careful around that one.

"Don't you worry about her," Hili whispered and patted my hand.

Who was I kidding? I looked around the room, taking in every single face that I didn't bother to notice the day before. Each of them was younger and way smarter in the magic department. Especially the Dark-Siders, which I knew nothing about. That wasn't going to stop me from finding out everything I could.

Helena cleared her throat. "As you all know, today is the day that Professor Sandlewood was going to announce who the intern will be this year."

A hushed excitement filled the air. This was the first time I had heard of any internship. Hili had her eyes closed and her fingers crossed in the air. She obviously knew what was going on and was praying it was her.

She opened her eyes and bounced up and down while her blonde razor-cut hair stayed tight to her head.

"Okay." Helena tried to settle down the electricity in the room. "Since Professor Sandlewood is a little incapacitated, I'll be picking the winner."

A little incapacitated? What was with all the secretive talk? Everyone knew about Eloise, so I found it strange that no one even mentioned it.

I raised my hand. Helena nodded toward me.

"I'm a tab bit confused. What is going on with Eloise and what is this internship thing?" These were valid questions for the new girl.

"Eloise will not be back this semester." Her lids darkened her cheeks, creating a scary shadow. "Every year we pick a student with exemplary grades as well as skills. This year Faith Mortimer was in the lead, but with her sudden illness, I'm going to have to pick Hili Windover."

"Ya hooo!" Hili jumped up and pumped her fist in the air. Never once letting go of her wand. As she bounced, sparks flew from the tip.

I shielded my face with my hand as Helena's words rang in my head. *Sudden illness.* I didn't realize that intentional poisoning had become a sudden illness. There was little room to think with Hili jumping around like one of those Mexican jumping bean toys I had when I was a kid. The ones that could be bought at the local gas station, in a little clear box.

"Hili, you will immediately be going to Whispering Falls since they have lifted the ban on Fairiwicks." She talked, but I couldn't quite focus on everything she was saying. "You have raised my eyebrow with your behavior last night, but I'm willing to give you a chance. And since June is here for a few days, you will go and work in her shop, A Charming Cure."

"What?" There was no way I was going to allow dingbat Hili to destroy my shop. I stood up and pounded my fist on the table, and then reached down in Hili's bag, holding up her soiled high-heeled shoe. "Aunt Helena, Hili is not a potion maker. She can't even keep her shoes on or prevent her little finger from sparking" I wiggled my finger in the air.

Helena put her hand in the air to silence me, but my words were like a spewing volcano.

"There is no way she will be able to come up with cures." Not to mention how Oscar was going to take it. He couldn't stand pretentious girls like Hili.

Helena pulled her crystal ball out from her bag that was sitting on Eloise's desk. With a swipe of the hand, a picture was appearing under the copper colored illumination. A Charming Cure was still in a disarray of sorts. A far cry from Oscar standing by the counter with my apron on.

"I see that you left your precious shop in the capable hands of a sorcerer that has never been to the University and doesn't even know how to use his wand." Her voice mimicked the pleasure on her face. "At least Hili can get the crowd under control and use her wand."

Hili nudged me. "I can't believe you don't trust me with your shop."

I turned toward her. "It's not that I don't trust you, it's just that you're young and you aren't psychic to what people really need in their cures."

"And he is?" Hili pointed to poor Oscar who had completely given up and planted himself on the stool behind the counter. His handsome features were already worn and his blue eyes even looked ashen. My apron was soiled with spilled potions.

"Fine." I glared, knowing that Oscar was going to be beside himself with little Miss Priss coming to take over.

"You screw something up and you will never practice your casting."

"Is that a threat?" Hili pulled back. Her eyes darted between me and Helena. "Did she just threaten me?"

"No. It's a promise." The words flew out of my mouth before I could stop them.

Hiss, hiss. Mr. Prince Charming ran into the classroom with his back arched and batted once toward Hili and once toward Helena.

Helena rolled her eyes.

"Hili will be fine, June. We all know how much you have worked on A Charming Cure and she is only going to see what it is like to run a business and see if she wants to continue down that path." *Swoosh, swoosh.* Helena's cloak created a breeze as she briskly walked up and down the aisle of the classroom. "Go on, Hili. Your transportation is waiting by the cottage dorm."

I wasn't sure who Helena was trying to convince, herself or me. She knew better than I did that Hili was incapable of doing anything with business. I was definitely going to have to get a hold of Oscar to let him know what was going on.

"Ta-ta." Hili grabbed her bag and waved over her shoulder. She didn't even look back as the door shut behind her.

The only good thing that could possibly come from this was that I could definitely keep working on a cure for Faith without anyone finding out.

"Since we are still looking for a replacement for Professor Sandlewood, we have decided to have you go to Crystal Ball Class early." Helena made her way back to the front of the room and carefully rolled her ball back and forth in her hands. She looked deep into the globe, her eyes grew big. "You are dismissed. Everyone but you." Her long finger uncurled and pointed straight at me.

Helena's eyes shot a dart straight to my gut, causing my lungs to take in a sharp breath.

Chapter Twelve

Every student filed out one-by-one with eyes on me. I was not making a good impression on my fellow students. Helena set my bag on the table.

"I sent someone to retrieve your bag from Hili's room." She stood over me. Her cloak hung loosely down from her folded arms.

A red glow came from my bag. I reached in and pulled out a pissed off Madame Torres. I set her next to me in case I needed some sort of backup with Helena after the class was gone. How on earth could a fiery red, mad crystal ball help? I had no idea, but there was a little relief knowing she had my back.

My stomach clenched as the boy who sat in the back of the class with his head down the entire time, left. He was the last to go, and I didn't know what Helena wanted with me.

Before leaving, he turned just enough for me to notice his white eyes. A flash shot through me, sending a small electric volt to my hands, causing me to let go of the edges. He smiled and darted out the door.

"Who was that?" I asked and pointed.

"Gus Chatham." There was a faraway look in her eyes. "A strange bird. But we aren't here to talk about him. You pulled a very serious stunt last night and I don't care if you are my niece. You are here as a student and will conduct yourself as one."

"You know as well as I do that Eloise didn't try to poison Faith." I stood up and planted my hands flat on the table. There was still a tingling on the tips of my fingers where Gus had done some sort of magic. Not sure what, but I was going to find out. He wanted me to know he had something to say, my intuition told me that. "And she doesn't deserve to be shackled."

She put her hand up to her mouth, and drew in a long breath. Her fists notably tightened.

"Oh my, God." Suddenly my intuition told me that Helena didn't know the full story. "Where is Eloise?"

Her head slowly dropped toward the ground, her eyes closed. Her confidence was broken, an attribute of hers that I'd never seen or even knew she possessed. She almost seemed human.

"That is another thing I was going to ask you about. You didn't take her from the holding cell?" She pinched her lips together. "I was afraid of this."

Suddenly my fear beaded across my forehead. I swept my bangs out of my eyes to wipe the sweat. Something was not right, and I was almost afraid to ask.

"Aunt Helena, what is going on?" I reached for Madame Torres. "Show me Eloise."

The globe went from her fiery red to silver, showing the ill-fated destination of Eloise chained to the wall. She rolled a small petal from a Mandrake flower in her fingers, as if were the only thing keeping her alive.

Helena withdrew her eyes from the globe once she saw the shackles, and her voice trembled, "She has been missing and we couldn't find her."

"You mean to tell me that you have all of this *magic* surrounding you and no one can find her? Someone kidnapped her?" I pounded my hand on the table.

"No." Shame, defeat resonated in her voice. "I was hoping that you found something in your snooping around. Even though I'm not condoning it in front of the other students."

"Actually, Madame Torres showed me Eloise. I snuck out to see if I could find something on my own." I wasn't sure if I should tell her about Raven and how she was in

Eloise's house. "Hili did tell me that Eloise was considered a Dark-Sider, which was complete news to me."

"Dark-Sider, or Good-Sider, either way, we are all here and living among each other. No one can come into Hidden Hall unless they are invited." She cleared her throat as her posture tightened. "Someone on the inside took her."

My heart jumped at a quick, erratic pace. "Do you think it was the same person that tried to set her up? The same person that tried to kill Faith Mortimer?"

Helena's eyes locked with mine. Never once looking away, she confirmed my deepest fear.

"Yes. And if you aren't careful, I'm afraid they will be after you." She pulled a piece of from underneath her cloak, and handed it to me.

> *Potions, wands, and fairy tales,*
> *Won't keep you safe as well.*
> *Eye of Newt won't be your friend,*
> *You're snooping around better end!*

"Where did you get this?" I could steady my quivering lip, but not my trembling chin.

"Gus found it on your bed while he was retrieving your bag." Her eyes widened.

"Gus? That strange bird is who retrieved my bag *from my room*?" I huffed and rolled my eyes.

"He's a Teletransport psychic, plus my assistant. Still a strange bird, but he gets the job done and is great at keeping secrets." She peered out the window. "He's on our side."

"You mean he can vanish into thin air, going from place to place?"

She nodded her head.

I was going to let that slide. . .for now. I tapped Madame Torres and Eloise reappeared. "You don't know where Eloise is? You don't recognize the room?"

She shook her head. "I banished her to the holding cell. Gus was there and left her alone while he scoured her house for anything. When he got back, she was gone."

"And what about all the magic ability here? Can't we find her? Can't anyone use their ability to find her?" This seemed like a pretty normal thing. After all, before I found my spiritual gift, I thought psychics could find out anything.

"That is not how all of this works. Whoever took her is good at making their magic tracks disappear. But my real question is why? Why did they harm Faith and why did they kidnap Eloise?"

Helena brought up some great questions that I wasn't able to answer. The person obviously wanted to kill Faith, but what good was it to keep Eloise chained up…or alive for that matter.

"I know I shouldn't be asking you to do this, and the campus police are doing everything they can to solve this crime. But you have more power than you know." Her voice was flat, monotone. She held a skeleton key from the tips of her fingers. I reached out and took the cold metal object; the eyes hollowed out were worn and tarnished. "This is the key to the student files. I'd love for you to use your intuition skills by reading through them. Maybe something or someone will catch your attention. Be sure not to get caught."

I gripped the key with an unsettled feeling in my gut. This was going to be much harder than I thought.

I tapped the crystal ball again, and Oscar appeared in the center of Charming Cure. Hili stood in front of him barking orders while pointing. He was putting bottles on their perspective shelves and nodded at each of Hili's commands.

"Well, at least I'm not going to have to worry about the shop." Glad that Hili was there, fixing all of the mishaps, I was going to be able to focus all my attention of finding two things. Find a cure for Faith. And finding Eloise.

"One more thing," I turned back around before I left. "What's the history between you and Gerald?"

A stark look crossed her face. Her scar turned a visible red, but the rest of her face stayed the same.

"Go." She drew her arm out from under her cloak and pointed to the door.

I did what she said, only for now. I would find out that secret too, one way or another.

Chapter Thirteen

I tucked the key in the front pocket of my jeans to make sure it was safe and sound, and then hurried off to crystal ball class. Helena had assured me that I wouldn't be in trouble for being late, and that she had Gus tell the professor that Helena was keeping me a bit after class.

"I hate being late." Madame Torres groaned from the depths of my bag.

Once I got to the arrowed signs in the middle of the wheat field, I tapped the arrow pointing toward Crystal Ball School and the field parted as it should, and lead me down the path.

At the end of the path stood three red-bricked buildings. Each one with a covered porch held up by four very tall pillars. A sign dangled from each stated the level of skill: beginners, intermediate, and advanced.

Obviously, I was a beginner. After all, Madame Torres seemed to run the show more than I did. That was a problem.

I took her out of my bag, and she appeared quicker than a jackrabbit. I held her up to eye level and gazed in. "Are you dressed up?"

Her red wavy hair was partially covered by a hot pink turban. Her eyelids smeared in purple eye shadow and lined in black liner didn't over power her long lashes that she batted words trickled out of her fire engine lips. "This is my time to shine. I'm single and ready to mingle."

"There will be no mingling." I assured her. "We are here on business. One, find out who poisoned Faith and two where they kidnapped Eloise. Plain and simple. *No mingling.*" I warned her, but knew I was talking into the air.

Granted, I knew I was here to go to school, but a lot can change in a couple of days.

"What can happen in four days?" I whispered under my breath and rolled my eyes as I pushed the door open to begin my first ever class of Crystal Ball School.

"Yep, yep, yep." The professor paced back and forth in front of the class. He wrung his hands and looked to the floor. His grey suit was much too big for his narrow shoulders, and much too long for his six-foot frame. The hem of his pants dragged the floor, and exposed only the tips of his black, soft-soled shoes. His jacket was hanging open and his white collared shirt was untucked and unevenly buttoned. He ran his hands through his thin, unruly hair and stopped pacing. Looking up, he pointed at me. "I heard about you, June Heal."

It didn't sound like a good 'heard' either. *Professor Dunwoody,* his name was scribbled on the chalkboard behind him.

He looked back down and started his pacing. His hands continued to wrap around one another. "Go on, take a seat."

I should've looked to see what seats were available before I jumped at the first one I came to. Madame Torres glowed a bright pink, and slightly rolled to the left side of the table toward my tablemate.

When I reached over to roll her back, I glanced up to see the person sitting next to me.

Gus.

He smiled. His crystal ball slightly rolled toward me and a man appeared in a turban. His eyes locked eyes with Madame Torres.

"Oh no you don't." I picked her up and placed her on my right side, out of sight of Rico Sauvé. I couldn't help but get the smooth singing Latino hunk out of my mind when I noticed Gus's crystal ball seemed to look a bit like a Latin lover. Tan, dark, and handsome.

"She was a little spitfire when I put her in your bag this morning." Gus swung his head to the right. His long blonde hair lay perfectly against his chiseled jaw line. I didn't realize the surfer dude look was still in. Nor did I ever imagine a spiritualist to have such a look.

"Tell me about it," I groaned and rolled my eyes. I turned my attention toward the professor.

He rambled on about the history of crystal balls and how they chose you, not the other way around. He talked about how obedient they were and accommodating. He'd obviously never met Madame Torres.

Nothing in my spiritual world was exactly like everyone else's, but that was okay. I was beginning to like my world. And that included Eloise. I felt my jean pocket to make sure the key was still there. After crystal ball class, I was going to muddle around the campus and take note on what everyone was doing and when a good time to snoop around would be.

"Miss Heal?" The professor brought me back from the land of daydreaming.

I sat up straight, and tall. "Yes." I answered without even knowing what he had asked.

"Well?" He stood still, his feet pointed outward making a V. "Can you tell us about it?"

About what? My nerves did summersaults on my stomach. I knew there was a reason I had never gone to college. Being called on in class was my worst nightmare.

"Tell us about how you found your crystal ball." He paced back and forth waving his hand in the air, never once looking at me.

With what seemed like a waste of precious time, I hurried through the story of how I had walked into Mystic Lights in Whispering Falls. Plus, I had no idea that I was a spiritualist when Madame Torres picked me.

With a few laughs and a smiling Madame Torres, class was over. With my back to Gus, I wanted to make sure Madame Torres made it back into my bag without a love connection.

"Wait." She begged, her eyes darted back and forth trying to see around my arm. But, I stuck her deep in the bag and strapped it over my shoulder.

As I gathered up my books, I heard some other students talk about getting lunch and a few were going to the library. It was lunchtime and I bet a lot of professors were also out eating.

"So what do you think about all the craziness since you came." Someone tapped on my shoulder. I turned around to find Gus and his goofy half-cocked grin standing behind me.

"Me? Since I came?" I put my hand up to my chest. Why, all of a sudden, did they think this started after I got here?

"Well, I did find that note and all." He shrugged and threw his crystal ball into his back pack like it was a baseball. "Aren't you a little old to be coming to school?"

"If you must know," I huffed. (*Old? When did twenty-five become old?*) "I had no clue I was even psychic until a few months ago. So I came here for a few days to learn all about it. But it looks like I'm going to be here longer."

There was no way I was leaving in a couple days with Eloise being kidnapped and Faith on her deathbed. There had to be something I could do.

The students filed out behind us, but not before I overheard someone say something about Faith not being able to put out the gossip paper.

"Did you hear about her nails?" A few students gathered around the gossiping one. "I heard that her dad put a spell around her. If an intruder comes in and tries to mess with her, her nails are full of poison and will strike."

"That's enough. Run along." Helena motioned for them to leave.

I couldn't help but smile when I heard the gossip about the nails. If only they knew. But the UnHidden Hall rag paper was another story. If Faith really were the master that uncovered the hidden truth behind the magic, it would open the door for many people who would want to hurt her. In fact, they might even want her dead.

Mr. Prince Charming came running in and made his signature figure eights around my ankles just as Gus was leaving.

"Where have you been?" I reached down and picked him up as though he was really going to tell me. Then I turned to Gus. "Are you walking back to the main campus?"

"Something like that." He threw his head back and laughed.

"Oh, I forgot. Teletransporter." *Damn!* Why couldn't I have that kind of power? Nonchalantly I asked, "So did you check out Faith's newspaper?"

His head gave a slight tick, and his eyes narrowed. "How did you know about that?" he asked, making it sound very suspicious.

"Doesn't everyone?" I laughed, shrugging off the ignorance. "Everyone knows its Faith, but won't admit it. Do you have any copies lying around?"

"Nope." He grabbed the edge of his backpack and right before my eyes, he was gone.

Hiss, hiss. Mr. Prince Charming jumped up on the table and batted at something that wasn't there. At least nothing I could see.

Faith Mortimer had pissed someone off and I wanted to read all of the newspapers. I grabbed Mr. Prince Charming off the table.

There was a piece of paper on the table that wasn't there before. I picked it up.

Meet me by the library in twenty minutes. Don't tell anyone! Gus.

I wondered why my hippie friend wanted to meet with me. What was so important that he couldn't tell me before?

I glanced around, wondering who else was in the room with me. I had a feeling I wasn't alone.

Chapter Fourteen

By the time Mr. Prince Charming and I got back to the main campus, it was time to meet Gus at the Library.

This better not be a waste of time, I thought. I really could've spent this time working on a new potion for Faith or going through her laptop. Or, I could've gotten into the files quicker. But I was going to take any tips I could use. And with Gus being able to go here and there without anyone seeing him, maybe he did see something.

The café shops were filled with students eating their lunch between classes, as well as professors grabbing a quick bite.

It was up to me to find out when it would be a good time to sneak in and take a peek at the student files. Maybe I could lurk around after I meet with Gus.

From a distance, I could see Gus was already there. His cargo shorts hung low like most the college boys were wearing them, and his t-shirt was ratty and halfway tucked in.

I thought about Oscar and smiled. He was always so neat. He liked his t-shirts wrinkle free, even though he didn't tuck them in. Oscar had a relaxed style and it worked for him. Gus on the other hand, was sloppy. Like most of the college boys at Hidden Hall.

"Hey, thanks for meeting me." Gus walked ahead is if I knew to follow him. "You know you shouldn't be going around asking about the newspaper thing."

"So now you admit to it?" I asked. He walked a few steps ahead of me and I tried to keep up. "Slow down."

Meowl, meowl. Mr. Prince Charming darted across the road to our cottage dorm. He must've been sick of listening to us, and didn't think I was in danger.

"No can do. If anyone sees me talking to you, they are going to know." He meandered a little further to the right.

"Know what?" I jutted forward. I looked around. No one seemed to pay any attention to us.

"Know that I'm Helena's assistant and that I'm talking to you." The closer I got, the quicker he got.

"No one knows? Why?" I questioned.

"I'm really not in school. I'm in disguise to make sure the University runs well." He continued to get faster and faster. "I'm the best Teletransporter in the spiritualist's community."

Wow! If Aunt Helena really wanted me to help, why hadn't she clued me in on all this? After all, she never told me that Gus wasn't a student and that he worked for Hidden Hall.

"The administration knew that a Dark-Sider was trying to get the Ultimate Spell, and UnHidden Hall came out with an issue a month ago saying that they knew who it was and was going to expose them in this month's issue. This month's issue was due out today. And it's not out, so we can all assume that Faith really does put out the paper."

Ultimate Spell? What the hell was that? I smacked my forehead with my hand. There was still so much I needed to learn. And why couldn't they know it? There was only one way to find out. . .ask.

"What's the Ultimate Spell?" I ran up next to him. In a flash, he was gone.

Damn it! I looked around to see if he Teletransported across the street or a little further up the sidewalk. The more I stood there and thought about it, the more I realized standing there was getting me nowhere.

A chill ran up my spine and a cold breeze brushed my cheek.

"Who's here?" I jumped around. My eyes darted into the air. I was not alone.

"Are you okay?" A girl asked as she walked by. She stood back as if I was just released from a psychiatric ward.

I brushed her off. "I'm fine, thanks."

She nodded and went on her way. I turned around and realized I was standing in front of the admissions office.

Gus had leaded me to the place I needed to be. Only I wanted to go back and raid Faith's computer to figure all of this out.

The sign on the door read that the administration was out for their lunch break and the office was closed.

"Ms. Heal." Professor Dunwoody came out of nowhere and cleared his throat. Suspicion crossed his gaze. "Can I help you with something? The building is closed."

I thrust my hand in my bag and felt around for a Ding Dong. Finally, I felt the foil and pulled it out. I made a mental note to replenish my stash when I got back to my room at the cottage.

"I'm just taking a look around at the beautiful campus." I took a bite to stall for time. "I never had the opportunity to go to college when I was younger. I love all of this old architecture."

"I guess I could let you in." He opened the front of his suit coat, and hooked on his belt was a bunch of dangling keys on one of those pulley-type key chains that janitors wear.

How many keys could one man have? I thought as I watched him open the door with what looked like a normal key, not a skeleton key like the one Helena gave me.

Quietly we passed several doors with leaded glass, a nameplate on the outside of each. Nothing sparked an interested or created a stir.

One door that did catch my eye was the one marked Basement. I eyed the old door and noticed the key hole didn't match the others. That was where my key went. Not only did my intuition tell me, but my bag glowed bright amber.

Madame Torres was well aware that the basement was where I needed to go.

The admissions office was just across the hall. A small wooden bench sat to the left of the door.

"I think I'll wait here until they get back from lunch." It groaned as I plopped down.

"Fine, suit yourself." Professor Dunwoody ran his hands through his hair, and then wrung them as he shuffled down the hall. Never once did he make eye contact with me.

If my timing was right, the staff wouldn't be back for another forty-five minutes, which gave me plenty of time to get to the basement. Probably not enough time to look through the student files, but I'd worry about that once I got down there.

I waited for a few minutes just in case Professor Dunwoody came back, but he didn't. I tiptoed over to the door and slipped the key out of my pocket.

"Here goes nothing." The key scrapped the edges, and let out a faint cry as if it hadn't been opened in quite a while. The door swung open without me forcing it. A rush of cold air swept up the dark wooden floors, causing my bangs to part in the middle.

Something didn't want me to go down there, but Madame Torres remained amber. I opened my bag to look in, hoping her glow would light up the inside of my bag and I could get another Ding Dong. There were none.

Madame Torres showed me a picture of Eloise hunkered over. Instantly my fear went away. I had to do this for Eloise. She had been there for Darla and me. I was going to find her and whoever had done this to her. As well as Faith.

Chapter Fifteen

The bare light bulbs hung from the ceiling with old tube and knob wiring, along with several cob webs, actually worked when I pulled the chain that hung from them.

Careful not to touch anything, I rubbed my owl charm that dangled off my bracelet between my fingers.

"Make wise decisions," I repeated over and over, hoping it would spark a little more courage in my gut. There was nothing telling me to turn around other than the pure scaredy-cat that I was.

I made it to the landing and peered down the other set of wooden steps. It was much darker than the first half of the steps and I didn't see any hanging bulbs. With a series of short breaths, I gained a little more courage and bolted down the steps.

I ran my hand up and down the wall looking for a light switch. It was cold and there was nothing there but dust. At the top was a stream of light, a small stream, but a stream no less. I felt my hand around toward the light and felt some sort of bag. I pulled the bag down, only to be covered in dust and a plume of it created a fog. I closed my eyes waiting for it to settle.

I squinted to see if the coast was clear and a light shone through. The bag had been covering a window to the street. I could see the student's feet as they walked by.

It was just enough light to see the many rows of filing cabinets that filled the large basement.

I reached in my bag and grabbed Madame Torres.

"Can you shine a light over there?" I held her up and she did exactly what I needed her to do. Thank God she didn't give me any fits. From the looks of it, she was about to take a nap. Regardless, I needed to see exactly who Faith Mortimer was and where she came from. There were many more families I wanted to look up, but surely there had to be something in Faith's past to lead me to a clue as to who she really is.

Why would she be best friends with a Dark-Sider when Raven clearly distastes Good-Siders? Did Raven have something against Faith in order for Faith to befriend a Dark-Sider?

"They are all alphabetized." She blurted out, and shone a light on the letter M.

"You knew exactly what I was thinking." I carefully made my way over the cabinet.

"This place gives me the heebie jeebies and I want to get out of here." She focused on the cabinet, lighting my way.

Stay focused, I repeated in my head because I knew I could easily get distracted. This place was definitely not somewhere I wanted to stay for a long period of time. Plus my time was limited. Eloise didn't look well.

I ran my finger down the drawers, looking for where 'Mortimer' would fall into the filing system. Luckily, it was the middle drawer. With a little extra pull, the drawer opened. With a little more effort, the drawer squeaked and was much too slow. I yanked harder and it opened a little quicker with just enough space for me to thumb through the old files.

A slight cold breeze blew at the nape of my neck, causing me to pause and look into the darkness behind me.

Stop it. You're overreacting, I told myself. Only, there was an unshakable sense of something wrong. With one hand in the files, I used the other hand to find a Ding Dong.

Damn! I had forgotten I was out. I turned my attention back to the files and quickly found a tab that had 'Mortimer' printed on it.

Using Madame Torres as a flashlight, I thumbed through the old papers briefly reading about Faith's family history. Flipping through, I stopped when a letter addressed to Aunt Helena caught my eye.

Dear Dean Helena Heal,

As you know, my daughter, Faith Hope Mortimer, will be attending Hidden Hall A Spiritualist University starting in the fall. We hope that our donation in the amount of one million dollars will go toward new and exciting research that will benefit Faith's educational career at Hidden Hall.

As you know, my wife and I value education as well as the internship program at Hidden Hall. We believe that Faith has a wonderful chance at obtaining the qualifications as the top student. As for other business we discussed on my last visit, I'm sure you have taken the necessary precautions to help keep the information sealed. Especially the Ultimate Spell situ…

"Especially the Ultimate Spell what?" I turned the page, but the proceeding pages had been ripped out of the file. It was gone. What was the other business he was talking about and what was the Ultimate Spell?

With the file back in place just like I found it, I slammed the old metal door shut.

"What have I gotten myself into?" I stared deep into Madame Torres eyes searching for answers she wasn't able to give me. Carefully I slipped her back in my bag and headed toward the stairs.

Chapter Sixteen

I slipped out of the administration office unseen and ran across the street to the cottage dorm.

First thing was first. I had to get on Faith's computer. Not only did I want to get my hands on the old editions of UnHidden Hall, but I wanted to figure out this Ultimate Spell. Why was it so secretive?

Everyone seemed to be out of the house, so I darted up the steps, and stopped when I heard a slight scuffle and door slam coming from the hallway. My hallway.

Hili was gone to Whispering Falls, and Faith. . .well, we knew where Faith was. So who was in my hallway and why?

The lights turned on like falling dominoes in the dark hallway as I rushed toward my room. The door was opened. I flipped on the light switch to a ransacked room. The contents of my desk drawers were emptied. The mattress was thrown on the floor as if I had something to hide between them, and the contents in my suitcase had been strewn about. Everything that I had purchased at Potions, Wands, and Beyond was gone.

"Oh my god!" I grabbed the box of Ding Dongs that was full when I left my room, but was now empty. "This is war. No one messes with my Ding Dongs."

I threw the empty box on the floor and ran into the hallway to see if I saw anyone, but there was no one there. Someone was looking for something or trying to send me a message. Wasn't the note enough?

I took the threatening note out of my back pocket and remembered that Helena had told me that Gus found it.

I plopped down on the jumbled up sheets on my bed where the intruder had ripped them off to read the note for the hundredth time hoping something…anything would pop out at me, but when I did, my heel hit something, causing that something to roll under the bed frame.

Bending down, I looked between my legs and saw a small bottle way under there that was slowly coming to a stop.

For a moment, it looked like it was one of the ingredients I had gotten from Potions, Wands, and Beyond, but the bottle was way too beautiful with the swirls of colors and a cork top.

I got on my belly and reached as far as I could. With a little luck, I turned my head to the side and slid just far enough under the frame for the tips of my fingers to reach it and roll it towards me.

With the bottle firmly in my grasp, I pulled myself out and bringing it to my face, got a closer inspection.

"Cimicifuga?" I read the label phonetically. "Cimicifuga, cimicifuga!"

I recalled the strange ingredient from spying on Raven that night.

Raven.

I grabbed my Magical Cures book from bag and quickly thumbed through it. Obviously Raven was the one who broke into my room, but why did she have the ingredient with her?

The ingredients were listed alphabetically as I ran my finger down each page, turning them when I reached the end. Finally, I made it to Cimicifuga.

"Black snakeroot." I quickly scanned the notes until I found out what it was exactly used for. "Ward off unwanted illness. Sprinkle on the floor for unwanted visitors. Get rid of evil jinx."

Meow, meow. Mr. Prince Charming tapped the bottle.

Was she trying to get rid of me? Or did she drop it when I unexpectedly came home? Was the potion really for

Faith? Was Raven on her way to finish Faith off after she found what she was looking for here?

More and more questions made my head foggy, only making me crave a Ding Dong even more.

I put the bottle in my bag for safekeeping. All my evidence was going to stay with me at all times. I couldn't risk anyone else coming in and ransacking the place again.

I quickly put everything back in its place, which didn't take too long since there wasn't much there to begin with. After all, it was only four days. . .*right!*

I dragged the chair underneath the air conditioning vent and quickly unscrewed it using the tip of my fingernail.

Luckily, the intruder, who I was sure was Raven, didn't think to look in the vent, because Faith's computer was still in there safe and sound.

My intuition told me I was going to have to use more than my psychic ability to solve this one.

Before I dug too deep into the Mortimer family history, I wanted to see exactly where Raven was and what she was doing. Maybe I could catch her fleeing from here. Or did she realize she had dropped her bottle on the way out? She'd be back for it, I just knew it. But when?

Madame Torres was deep in the bottom of my bag. I pulled her out and gently tapped the glass with my fingernail.

Nothing.

I tapped again, this time a little harder.

Still nothing.

With both palms securely around the globe, I shook it.

"Whoa!" Madame Torres gave off her 'I'm mad' red glow. "I'm not one of those toy eight balls. And you can't shake me until you get the answer only you will accept."

"Flea market!" I shouted back.

"Fine, what do you seek?" She asked.

"I want you to show me Raven." That was it. I was sure she'd be running back into the woods by now.

"No can do."

"Yes can do." I repeated back to her. "There is no time to be snarky, Madame Torres. I demand to see Raven."

"You don't understand." Madame Torres' demeanor had suddenly saddened. "Raven has put a block up. She has figured out a way to void her of any tracking."

Defeated, I put Madame Torres back on the nightstand. "Dark-Sider," I murmured, wishing that I knew a little bit more about them.

There had to be something on the computer that gave a clue to who had done this.

"Hmm." The computer started up quickly. "I guess when you have money, you can afford the top-of-the-line laptop."

I scanned through her documents, but there were only notes from classes. Her picture folders were empty as well as the other folders, which made me believe that the University police had already swiped the laptop clean. No wonder it was still in her room.

My intuition told me to stick with what I was good at to solve this crime. . .cures. Plus, I had to beat Raven on whatever potion she was working on.

So I closed the laptop to focus on a new potion to help Faith come out of the sleep and tell us what was going on. If she did wake up, she'd be able to tell us that Raven was the Dark-Sider who wanted to find out the Ultimate Spell.

Thinking about the reaction Faith had to the first potion, and since it only made her nails come back to life, maybe I could bring her back to life potion-by-potion, starting with her respiratory system. If she can breathe on her own, maybe her other functions would start as well.

Chapter Seventeen

"You are doing a lot of homework for only being in for two days." The cashier at Wands, Potions and Beyond slowly scanned the new ingredients.

"Umm, hmm." I tried not to look at her. She obviously knew the rule was that we weren't allowed to work on any potions that weren't class related.

"What class is it again?" The whites of her eyes were bright against her fair skin and purple hair. Her fingers with black nail polish on the tips picked up the last bottle and she read the label.

"Nux Vomica. I don't recall using that as a beginner."

"Just put it in the bag." I ordered her. So what if it was the root of a poison nut. It was used for all sorts of cures according to my Magical Cures Book.

"Whatever," she growled. Her eyes stared over top her heavily blackened eyeliner. "All you Good-Siders are alike." She dangled the Wands, Potions, and Beyond bag on her finger. I went to get it and her finger curled around the handle. "Your intuition is way off."

I grabbed the bag and headed straight out the door. That was the problem. My intuition wasn't working at all.

"Why so gloom?" I jumped around flinging my sack in the air as Gus ducked to miss a hit square in his pretty little jaw bone. "Whoa!"

"You scared me! You can't go around teletransporting yourself into my business or life." I stomped across the street to the cottage dorm. Gus followed. "You can't come in here."

"Want to bet?" He disappeared.

"Whatever!" I yelled into the night sky hoping he could hear me.

Without looking at anyone, I darted up the stairs and back into my room to find Mr. Prince Charming nestled in Gus's arms as they sat on my bed.

"Told you I could get in here." He stroked Mr. Prince Charming.

"Traitor," I mumbled under my breath when Mr. Prince Charming looked up at me.

I threw the bag of ingredients on the desk and plopped down on the little couch.

"So you *are* snooping?" His dark snappy eyes looked at me. "Your Aunt is not going to like this."

"Is that so?" I reached for the bag and took the bottles out setting them next to my little cauldron. "She hasn't been so forthcoming with me either, and needs to be; especially if she wants me to look into a few things."

"She what?" He darted up and Mr. Prince Charming shot off his lap. "What do you mean?"

"She gave me the key to the administration building so I could use my intuition skills to figure out who had done this to Faith. Only. . ." I hesitated and tapped on Faith's laptop that was still on my desk. "Someone had already gotten to the file and ripped out the important page."

The cauldron gave off a couple puffs of smoke.

"Come on." I waved my hand for him to follow me. I needed to go back over to Faith's room and get the pop can out of the trash so I could salvage any type of spit. That would be great for a respiratory cure.

I grabbed the laptop to put it back.

"You can get kicked out for that too." He gestured to the pink laptop.

"Not mine. Faith's. It seemed she broke a lot of rules and never got in trouble with the University." It was true. Faith had broken a lot of the University rules, but her daddy's money probably paid for a lot of people to overlook things. Only someone didn't overlook something and left Faith to die.

"Eww. . .Why are we coming in here?" He drew back
with a twisted look on his face and pointed to Faith's name
on the door.

"I'm the one who gave Faith the cure that made her
nails come back to the living." I reached in the wastebasket
and grabbed the can. "I can't figure out a full cure to bring
her back, so I'm going to do it little-by-little."

Amusement danced across his face. He flipped his
head to the side; his shaggy mop settled into a mess on top
his head. "You are a clever one." He shook his finger at
me.

Slipping back out of Faith's room, we went back to
mine where I began Faith's new cure.

"Your Aunt is really not going to like this. It can get
you kicked out." Gus watched as I threw in a pinch of the
Nux Vomica, and then he quirked back when the flames
shot up in the air.

"It's fine. Just stand back." I assured him. "Quite
frankly I didn't care if Helena kicked me out or not. What
is it going to do to me? Not let me take over Whispering
Falls Village Council President when Izzy retires? Whoop-
dee-doo."

"What are your thoughts on who is doing it?" Gus asked.

"My initial thought is Raven, but things don't add up." I told him about the pictures of her and Faith, plus how they seem to be good friends. "I did find this."

I threw the little potion bottle that Raven had accidentally left behind after she ransacked my room.

A shocked look crossed his face.

"I think she was trying to send me a warning signal." I shrugged. "Don't get me wrong. I care about Faith, but I really want to find Eloise."

Recalling her in the shackles made me work quicker on the respiratory cure.

The thin substance that rose in the cauldron with gray oddiments smelled like mud and a mixture of blueberries.

"Thank you," I whispered under my breath. There was a scent. A strange combination, but still a smell. The last potion I made for Faith was odorless.

This gave me a little hope that she was coming back to us and soon Eloise would be too.

"This is crazy." Gus gushed as the liquid oozed out of the cauldron and dropped into the small opening of the can. "They never let this cool stuff happen here."

"If you think this is nuts." I shook the can in front of his face. "What until you see what happens when I give it to Faith."

"Cool. I'll meet you there." Gus turned to disappear.

"Wait!" I put my other hand out. "I want you to Teletransport and let me know if the coast is clear. I don't want anyone seeing us."

He nodded. Then he was gone.

Chapter Eighteen

The coast was clear as I made my way into Faith's hospital room. Gus wasn't there as far as I could tell, but that didn't mean he wouldn't be showing up at any time.

Mr. Prince Charming hopped up on Faith's bed.

Meowl, meoowl. He touched Faith's cheek with his paw.

"I know, buddy. I wish she'd wake up too." I rubbed my hands down his back while I looked over Faith's body. There was no change. Only her fingernails were perfect, just like the old Faith. "Here goes nothing."

Just like I had done yesterday, I parted her lips with one of my hands and tipped the pop can into the open space.

The potion was thick like honey and it took me a few shakes of the can to get one big drip out. I backed up shielded my eyes. There might be another crazy explosion like the previous reaction and I wanted to be prepared.

Beep, beeeeeep, beep, beeeeeep, blip, blip, beeeeeeeeeeeeeeeeeeeeeeeeeeeeeeeeeeeeeep!

"Oh, no you don't." I ran over and looked at the monitor that was hooked up to her. "No, no, no."

I grabbed Faith by the shoulders and jerked her up and down, before I heard footsteps running down the hall.

Hiss, hiss. Mr. Prince Charming jumped down and took our rightful hiding place under the hospital bed. Taking a cue from him, I threw myself on the ground and rolled under. We were getting really good at this.

Please no, please no. I begged with my eyes squeezed shut. Did the potion kill her? The last thing I needed was to be marked a murderer. . .again.

This spiritualist lifestyle was proving to be very difficult.

"Get the cart!" The nurse screamed out of the door when she noticed Faith had flat-lined. "She's stopped breathing!"

A slew of nurses came running, filling the room. All of them shuffled around. They must've been doing a lot of poking and prodding because I could hear the clicking of a lot of buttons.

"Stand back!" I heard the male voice demand the nurses to move. He shouted, "Clear!"

Thump, thump. The bed bounced up and down with each shock of the paddles the doctor had placed on Faith.

"Clear!" He screamed again.

Beep, beep, beep, beep.

"Wait." He ordered. All the shoes that were lined up around the bed took a step back. Everyone made an audible, deep gasp. "This is a miracle. I need to know exactly what happened leading up to her cardiac arrest."

The nurses gave a brief overview of how everything played out, only they left out the little bit of magic they didn't know about. . .which was just fine with me! The less anyone knew the better for me.

"Well, it just goes to show how the body reacts. She seems to be responding to the respirator again." The doctor seemed proud of himself. "Let's check her stats."

Beep, beep, blip, blip, beep, beep. There was some inconsistency to the machine's noises.

"Doctor, I think she's breathing on her own." The nurse's shoes were a little too close to the edge of the bed. Granted, the life support machine was right up against the wall, just inches from my head.

I tilted my head to the side to make sure the toe of the nurse's shoe didn't accidently hit me.

"I think you are right." The doctor shuffled over. *1, 2, 3, 4. . .*I counted the shoes. There were a few clicks. "There are some irregular breathing patterns."

My heart nearly leapt out of my chest when I felt someone's hand wrap around my mouth and it wasn't a fury paw.

"Nice." Gus whispered in my ear. My heart eased a little when I realized it was him. "I think the potion did it."

"You freaked me out." I mouthed and put my finger up to my mouth to shush him. Mr. Prince Charming even knew better than to purr.

"Let's go ahead and shut off the machine and see if she picks up on her own." The doctor's voice broke with huskiness. There was a little apprehension in his tone.

"Are you sure, doctor?" The nurse questioned his actions.

"We have to try. If she doesn't pick up in fifteen seconds, we will turn the machine back on." The doctor wasn't leaving much room for Faith's body to respond. "Ready?"

The nurse must've gestured yes, because the next thing that was heard was the flat-line of the machine.

Beeeeeeeeeeeeeeeep.

I squeezed my eyes shut. I couldn't bear to hear the beep. I put my fingers in my ears to keep the noise out, but the doctor made me put my hands back to my side.

"1, 2, 3, 4, 5." He slowly counted, "6, 7, 8, 9, 10, 11, 12, 13, 14, 15. Let's turn the machine. . ." The doctor stopped in mid-sentence.

Beep, beep, beep, beep. The steady heartbeat, Faith's steady heartbeat picked up, creating the nurses and doctor to cheer.

"Amazing." The doctor's toes were pointed under the bed. He looked like he was checking out all her vital signs. "Everything looks great. Just keep a close eye on her. I'll go inform Dean Heal and the University Police."

The doctor walked out of the room.

"I've never seen anything like it." One nurse said to the other. "I'll go ahead and take the tubes out, while you clean up the tape marks."

I glanced over at Gus and he was gone.

"Let's go get a new set of pajamas for her." The nurses rushed out of the room, leaving Mr. Prince Charming and me alone.

Mr. Prince Charming ran out from under the bed and I rolled out, only to find Gus standing over Faith's bed.

"Wow, now that's magic." Gus leaned forward and lowered his voice, "You are *good*. Better than your Aunt."

My gentle laugh rippled throughout the air.

"Don't tell her I said that." He smiled. "Can I tell Faith I was a part of this?"

Faith's chest rose up and down with each breath she took. Her natural color was coming back to her face. The dark circles under her eyes had lightened up to a light shade of gray.

"Why, Gus, are you in love with Faith Mortimer?" Not only did I notice the love-struck look on his face, but my intuition told me he was pining over her. "You know I have a cure for that." I winked.

"Isn't she the loveliest spiritualist you have ever seen?" He reached out and touched her.

"Come on, we have to go before Aunt Helen gets here." I pulled his sleeve. Before I could let go, he was gone.

Quietly Mr. Prince Charming and I slipped out exactly the way we had gotten in. . . unseen.

Chapter Nineteen

There was a flurry of activity going on outside the hospital. Word had already gotten around that Faith was breathing on her own. Too bad I couldn't take the credit for it.

"June?" Aunt Helena lowered her gaze in confusion. "What are you doing here?"

Hiss, hiss. Mr. Prince Charming batted at her, and then darted off toward the cottage dorm.

"Stupid cat." She scowled. "I asked you a question."

"I. . ."

"She came to meet me for a drink." Gus stood next to me and pointed to Black Magic Café. "She has to have some social life while she's here."

"Good. I'm glad to see you getting out." She clenched her mouth tighter. "Carry on." She glided into the hospital. The automatic doors shut behind her.

Almost immediately the police had the door blocked off, not letting anyone in.

"What about that drink?" I reminded Gus of the promise he made Aunt Helena. "You might not be able to have a real drink, but I can and I need it."

Hopefully the café wouldn't be crowded, since everyone seemed to be gathered around the hospital, waiting on some news from Helena on Faith's condition.

"Fine." Gus walked down the street toward the café and I followed.

Black Magic Café was very intriguing with picnic tables throughout the green clapboard house scattered around to create seating. The wall behind the counter was made of chalkboard with all the items from the menu written on it.

"Hey, Gus." The young man behind the counter stuck his hand over the display case of cupcakes and they did some sort of guy handshake. "Want your usual?"

"You know it." Gus flipped his hair to the side. "This is June Heal."

The guy tipped his head back as if he was saying hi. Politely I smiled. My intuition told me that he already knew who I was. If not, The few customers that were in the café stared at me, and then followed by a few whispers.

"Make it two." Gus held up two fingers. "I always get the red velvet cupcake and tall glass of milk."

"Fine." It did sound good, but a real adult cocktail sounded better with a Ding Dong.

While Gus waited at the counter, I took a seat at the closest picnic table that wasn't taken.

"Well, well, well." The voice was firm. "If it's not the little goody niece."

"Get out of the way." Gus shoved past the girl who was the cashier from Wands, Potions, and Beyond.

"Shut up, Gus." She glared at him with her hands planted on her hips. "You would befriend her."

He sat the plates on the table before going back to get the milk.

"Ignore Tilly. She's bitter that *she* didn't get the internship." He laughed in her face.

"Whatever. Ignore him, Tilly." Raven appeared behind Tilly and put her hand on Tilly's shoulder. "Let's grab that table over there."

"Why aren't you at the hospital with your dear friend Faith?" My eyes clung to hers, analyzing her reaction.

"What are you talking about?"

"Faith is supposedly breathing on her own."

"I don't believe you."

"Of course you don't want to believe me because the little spell you put on her isn't working." I stood up and came nose to nose with the Dark-Sider.

"Are you accusing me of something?" She shoved me and I fell backwards onto the picnic table.

"Girls!" Aunt Helena appeared out of nowhere. "Stop it this instance. The University does not tolerate violence of any kind."

"Or potion making either." The girl from Wand, Potions and Beyond stepped in between Raven and me. "That is exactly what she's doing, Dean Heal."

"What?" Aunt Helena's eyes were sharp and assessing. "Don't tell me you broke a rule and have been making potions in your room."

"Dean." Gus tried to interrupt. "Dean… June. . ."

"Yes!" The girl screamed and pointed. "She has bought all sorts of non-related ingredients and a cauldron over the past twenty-four hours."

"June, is this correct?" Helena held her hands out to stop Gus from talking. The café fell silent, even the background music had been turned off. Everyone's eyes were on me. "Well?"

"Yes." There was no reason to lie. If I did, she'd only go to my room in the cottage dorm and find all the stuff. "But she broke into my room." I pointed to Raven hoping to get her in a little bit of trouble.

Raven stared with her mouth open.

"Did you not realize I knew it was you when you left your little bottle of this behind?" I took the bottle out of my bag and held the Cimicifuga in the palm of my hand.

"Where did you get that?" She set her chin in a stubborn line.

"June, Raven reported her homework missing earlier." Lines of confusion deepened along Helena's brows and under her eyes. "June Heal, I hereby expel you from Hidden Hall A Spiritualist University until further notice, not only for making potions that aren't school related, but stealing another student's homework."

Raven grabbed the bottle from my palms, scrapping a little of my skin off with it.

"But I didn't steal it! I found it under my bed after my room had been ransacked." I protested, but it was too late. A couple of Hidden Hall police officers grabbed me and escorted me out before I could prove my innocence.

Chapter Twenty

"Now what?" I slumped down on the bed and rubbed my hand down Mr. Prince Charming's back. I was very aware of the policemen standing outside of my room waiting to escort me back to the wheat field.

I was not only a disgrace to my Aunt Helena; I hadn't discovered who had poisoned Faith or any closer to finding Eloise.

Meow, Meow. Mr. Prince Charming jumped off the bed and did figure eights around my ankles. He was right; everything was going to be okay.

Maybe it wasn't a bad thing that I wasn't going to be finishing up my last couple of days at Hidden Hall. After all, I could work on a potion for Faith and get some help from my friends in Whispering Falls.

The suitcase was a little heavier since I had packed the extra things I had bought from Wands, Potions, and Beyond. With my purse over my shoulder and Madame Torres snug at the bottom, Mr. Prince Charming and I shut the door to our room.

"Goodbye." I said to each retired professor that was framed on the wall. Even though they couldn't talk, they still followed me with their eyes. Or did they? Their eyes darted back and forth between the ends of the hall as if they were trying to tell me something. Each had a deep-set fear. They were trying to tell me something, but what? "I'm sorry. I don't know what you are trying to tell me."

"Go!" The policeman stood behind me ordering me down the steps. "Your days of trying to solve crimes are over. Leave it up to the police, Ms. Heal."

Whatever. With no thanks to them, I heaved the suitcase down the stairs. All the girls, who were never home before, were home now. They didn't turn their accusing eyes away from me.

I tucked my hair behind my ears and with my head held high, I stepped out into the street and headed toward Whispering Falls. The girls in the cottage dorm weren't the only ones with curious eyes. What felt like the entire University population stood on the side of the road staring at me and Mr. Prince Charming as we made our walk of expelled shame, only it wasn't the shame that made me pause and turn around to look. It was my intuition telling me that I was missing something to help free Eloise.

The sky turned gray above the library, which was always sunny.

A hushed silenced blanketed the crowd as we watched the gray sky form clouds in the shape of a cleaning bottle.

Cleaning bottle?

I stopped dead in my tracks. Eloise's cleaning bottle. My stomach churned with anxiety and frustration on what the cleaning bottle symbol meant. Why couldn't I figure this out? There seemed to be many clues, but none of them made sense.

Just like the cloud appeared, it disappeared. The dark sky parted and the sun was once again bright and shining over the Once Upon A Time Library.

Chapter Twenty-One

Relief and happiness didn't fill my soul once I found my way around the Gathering Rock in Whispering Falls. In a few short minutes, I'd be at the clearing just behind my house with the town in the view, but it didn't make me feel right.

Something was wrong. Eerie and sadness blanketed the air like thick heavy wool. Yes, something was not right.

"June?" Izzy stood by the rock where the villagers always gathered in times of celebration and joy. "You're home?"

Izzy ran over with her arms stretched out. Her long blonde hair hung like spaghetti down each shoulder. Not the vibrant blonde I had left a couple days ago.

"I got expelled." I fell into her arms and she embraced me. "What are you doing here?"

I pulled away. There was a tired, weary look that was deep rooted in her eyes.

"I'm tired. I think I'm coming down with the flu or something." She bent down and picked up Mr. Prince Charming, who was doing figure eights around her ankles. "Plus I was showing Hili the way back to Hidden Hall."

"Hili?" I had completely forgotten about her. I couldn't wait to get back to the shop. "Why don't you stop by the shop later and I'll have a cure for that flu."

"That would be great. We really have missed you around here." She squeezed my hand. "Now, tell me how you got expelled!"

"That doesn't matter." There was no easy way to tell her about Eloise. They had been friends for years. "What matters is that Eloise has been kidnapped."

Izzy drew her hand up to her mouth. She hesitated, blinking with bafflement.

"Eloise had given a student in the class a dose of sleeping spell and it was laced with something that almost killed the student." I shook my head. "Aunt Helena put Eloise on administrative leave, but before the police could question her, someone kidnapped her."

"Oh my," her voice died away.

"I've been spending all my free time working on a potion to bring Faith back to life, but nothing seems to work." I looked out over Whispering Falls. The sky was different. It didn't seem to be as blue as it was before I had gone off the school. Shaking it off, I continued to tell Izzy what had happened with Faith and all the things I had found out.

"Faith?" Izzy's brows formed a V. "Faith who?"

"Mortimer." Izzy current state of health concerned me. She was visibly weak. She moved much slower than before. "I'm going to drop my suitcase off at home and then get to the shop to work on a cure. I have to bring Faith out of her coma and get the truth out of her before it's too late. Don't forget to stop by."

We hugged and I rushed back to my house to drop off my luggage with Mr. Prince Charming leading the way.

Chapter Twenty-Two

Before I set out for my shop, I grabbed my cell and called Oscar. He didn't answer, so I thought I'd surprise him with a visit.

Fear and anxiety wove in my soul as I made my way to A Charming Cure. The air was thick and mucky. Whispering Falls wasn't the same. The grass wasn't the Kentucky bluegrass I was used to. It was more like the Mojave Desert kind of grass, if there was any grass there.

I'm sure it was my imagination.

Belle's Baubles was shut tighter than a tick when I peeked in the window. There wasn't a sign on the window, so I was sure that Belle had gone to get a cup of tea over at The Gathering Grove.

I wasn't in the mood for tea, really not in the mood for anything. I had to figure a way to get back into Hidden Hall and find Eloise, but not without a cure for Faith.

"You're back a day or two early," Gerald stood behind the counter in his top hat. He twirled his mustache with one hand while pouring a cup of tea with the other. "The flu is going around."

"Is that why Belle Baubles is closed?" I pointed toward the village astrologers shop. It saddened me to see the village in a sick state.

"Yes." He shook his head. "Even poor Izzy can't shake it. I've been delivering tea to them every night."

"How long has this been going on?"

"A couple days," he shrugged, "since you've been gone." He handed me a cup of tea.

"Can I get it to go?" I wanted to make my rounds before I go to A Charming Cure to work on Faith's cure. "And one more thing."

He held the to-go cup with curiosity in his eyes over the counter.

"What is the history between you and my Aunt?" I reached for the cup just as he let go and it spilt all over the counter.

"Er. . .er. . ." He turned around and made another cup. But he sat it on the counter this time. "On the house. I've got to help the other customers."

He rushed off and helped the only other person in the shop. My eyes lowered and I bit my lip. It might not be as life threatening as figuring out where Eloise was, but it was definitely a piece of my life puzzle that I needed to know. My intuition told me so.

With my cup in hand, I trotted down Main Street looking at all the cozy shops. I missed Whispering Falls, but it wasn't the same without Eloise.

"You're back!" Petunia Shrubwood waved me down from the front of Glorybee Pet Store. Neatly tucked in her messy up-do was a chipmunk. I pulled back when she went to hug me. "Oh it's Henry. He's harmless."

She hugged me anyway.

"Why are you back so soon?" She tilted her head. Her normally vibrant chaotic locks were a little duller. And I could've sworn I saw a gray hair or two or ten. But, I wasn't going to tell her that.

"Are you feeling okay?" I wanted to make sure I wasn't going to dump all the news on someone who wasn't in tiptop psychic shape.

"Oh fine." She waved me off and invited inside the shop.

There wasn't a stray animal around Whispering Falls. They were all living in Glorybee with Petunia. The smell of animals hit me when I walked past the heavy electric blue wood door Petunia held open. I loved the big door with wavy yellow metal detailing that resembled the branches of a tree. Every single shop in Whispering Falls had an amazing door with details about what the shop had in store for you when you walked in.

The animals scattered across the floor. Some ran up the tree, while others ran into the burrows that were dug in the grass floor.

"Oh, it's just June." Petunia moved a little slower than normal.

"Are you sure that you are okay?" I helped her sit in the chair.

"I've been a little tired." Her eyes bordered with tears. "It's the strangest thing. I've done nothing different, but my energy is gone."

As if time had been sped up, Petunia had aged in the few minutes that I was there. There was no time to waste. Something bad was happening. Was there a correlation between what was going on with Hidden Hall?

"Did something happen in the spiritual world that we don't know about?" A hot tear dripped down her cheek. "There is something evil in the air. I just can't figure it out. Even the teenagers aren't roaming at night." She looked off into the distance. A blank stare on her face.

I swallowed hard, trying to manage a feeble answer, but nothing would come out. Hili must've been close to discovering the Ultimate Spell.

Was the Ultimate Spell the demise of the entire spiritualist world?

Chapter Twenty-Three

Walking over to A Cleansing Spirit Spa, I held out a little hope that my intuition was wrong and Chandra was her happy, spry, palm-reading self that was not a bit sick.

Standing between A Cleansing Spirit and A Charming Cure, I glanced over at the police station to see if there were any lights on over there. It was dark too, just like most of the shops were. Oscar's apartment was in the back of the police station, so maybe he was there.

I'm sure he was going to show up at some point. When he got my message, he'd know I was home.

"What do you mean you don't know?" The customer that sat in the chair in one of Chandra's manicure stations jerked her hands free from Chandra just as I walked in.

The bell above the door jingled when I entered, but that didn't detour the customer from jumping up and yelling.

"Since when do you *not* give advice?" The woman's face contorted, and she shook her fist in the air. "I come in here and don't want your unsolicited advice, and when I do come in here to get your advice, you don't give it?"

"I'm sorry," Chandra mumbled. Her turban was slightly tilted to the right. She definitely wasn't her jolly self.

"This will be the last time I come here for these overpriced manicures." The customer stomped past me and then stopped. She looked me square in the eye. "Don't waste your money."

*Don't let the door hit you where the. . .*I wanted to yell, but I didn't. Instead, my friend needed to be comforted.

Chandra put her hands in her face and began to sob.

"June, I'm so glad you are back." Her words were barely audible between her gasps and sobs. "Something has been horribly wrong around here. Everyone is getting some kind of flu; my psychic gift is completely off, if not gone."

She covered her face again. Her normally perfect manicured nails were chipped and ragged.

"Oh, Chandra." I bent down and embraced her. "I wish I could stay longer, but I need to go check on the shop. I promise you will be feeling better in no time."

I stood up. It probably wasn't the best time to leave a friend in need, but what she and the rest of Whispering Falls needed was me coming up with a cure to this problem. A problem that I was sure had to do with Raven, Faith, and Eloise.

"June," Chandra stopped me before I shut the door. "For some strange reason, I believe you."

"Believe me?" I wasn't sure what she was talking about.

"When you said I'd be feeling better in no time. I believe you. I believe in you." Her words hung between us. We both knew that what she just said had everything to do with….*magic.*

I nodded and left, heading next door to A Charming Cure.

"I'm so glad I ran into you." Mr. McGurtle stood at the front door with his hand. "I've been banging for ten minutes!"

Mr. McGurtle was back to his grumpy old self.

"How was your trip?" I used my key to open the door. The wonderful scents of jasmine, cinnamon, sage, mandrake, and all spice circled around our heads when we walked in.

I flipped the light on. A Charming Cure was in one piece but not in the best of shape. The display tables were sparse with very few bottles on each. The tiered dishes where all the homeopathic soaps were stood empty and the ingredients that lined the shelves behind the counter were either empty or half-full.

"Oh, no." Mr. McGurtle shook his head and ran his hand down his face.

I didn't know what he was talking about, but I did know it wasn't good. I reached behind the partition and took a Ding Dong from my stash.

Offering Mr. McGurtle half, I reluctantly asked, "Do I want to know what you are talking about?"

If anyone knew anything, it was Mr. McGurtle. For a man, he was the nosiest one I had ever met.

I took Madame Torres out of my bag and put her on the stand on top the counter.

Mr. McGurtle looked into the ball.

"Boo!" Madame Torres suddenly appeared, sticking her tongue out. "Miss us?" She cackled and the ball went black.

"Crazy old ball." He threw his hands in the air and paced back and forth.

I ignored them and walked down the line of ingredients, touching each bottle. There were more important issues than to warn Mr. McGurtle and Madame Torres to play nice.

Trickle, trickle. The sound of the ingredients filling up behind me as I went down the line was magic to my ears.

"Are you not worried about the state of the spiritualist society?" Mr. McGurtle stepped in front of me. His thin fingers pushed up his wide-rimmed black glasses upon his wide nose. His blue round eyes bore deep into my soul. "We have to talk about the Mortimer's. Faith and Raven Mortimer to be exact."

Chapter Twenty-Four

"Raven Mortimer?" I put my hand behind me, luckily catching the counter. If I hadn't grabbed the counter, I would've been face first on the floor from the shock that Raven's last name was Mortimer.

"Yes, yes. The Mortimer sisters." His stubby legs looked even shorter in his suit. He'd been away on business, not sure what type of business, but he always wore a suit when he was on business. "When I got Izzy's call this morning about you being expelled and Faith Mortimer's condition, I knew that Henry D. Boyle was going to have to wait."

"Henry D. who?" Mr. McGurtle was very good at talking in circles.

"Henry D. is the little boy I'm working with that is half Fairiwick, half mortal, sorta like you." He wrung his hands together. Mr. McGurtle had lived next door to me and Darla in Locust Grove. I didn't know it until a couple months ago that my pain-in-the-ass neighbor was really a spiritualist, that was ordered to move to Locust Grove and watch over us. No wonder he was always in my business. He would give monthly reports to the Whispering Falls council about me. When Darla died, he became especially nosey.

After I took over A Dose of Darla at the flea market, I began doing my own potions in the shed outside of our home. Mr. McGurtle was always calling Locust Grove police on me; luckily, Oscar was the one who always had to come bail me out from under Mr. McGurtle's wrath.

That was when Mr. McGurtle knew I had the spiritualist in me. He reported back to the council and Izzy showed up at my door. The rest was history.

"As if being expelled wasn't enough. Poor Darla. Love her soul." He did a sign of a cross and kissed his fingers before he shoved them toward the sky as if he was blessing poor Darla.

Poor Darla?

"Great! You have no idea what went on to get me expelled." I grabbed another Ding Dong. There was no way I was going to share with him this time. The nerve. "I was trying to save Faith Mortimer!"

"Well, we can't fight about that now. We have to do something to get you back to Hidden Hall." He pulled out a toothpick from his pocket and with a flick of his hand, the small piece of wood grew into a wand. "I'm a sorcerer that can get you back in, once we have figured out what's going on."

I didn't understand a word he was saying and didn't try to figure it out. Some things in Whispering Falls you just accepted as real. This was one of those things.

"I can tell you what's going on." Now I knew the truth behind the Mortimer sisters. I licked out the white creamy middle from my Ding Dong. "Raven is jealous of her sister. She is the one that wants the Ultimate Spell and she would stop at nothing to get it. Even trying to kill her own sister."

I wasn't sure how Eloise fit in, but she did. . .somehow.

"I knew you going to that school was going to make you even crazier." He babbled on about how I had innate intuition and that you couldn't teach the real thing.

"Oh shut up and figure this out," Madame Torres shouted from the counter.

"Grrrr…" Mr. McGurtle snarled and picked Madame Torres up and rolled her around.

"Umm. . ." I took her back and placed her back on the stand. "I wouldn't do that. She gets sea-sick."

I looked in and there was a scene of a tumultuous ocean swirling and twirling around. A sure sign Madame Torres was sick.

"Doesn't she have an off button?" He pointed his wand toward her. "I can shut her up!"

"No!" I shouted and threw myself in front of her. "This will get us nowhere. You obviously know that Eloise is missing and we need to find her."

Slowly he waved the wand back to toothpick size and put it back in his pocket. "I'll deal with *her* later. Besides, you are wrong about Raven Mortimer. She'd never hurt her sister."

My wide-eyed expression was merely a smoke screen. "How do you know the Mortimer's?"

"I watched over that family when they went on vacations." He looked off into the distance and smiled. "I recall how important it was for the family to incorporate the Good-Siders and Dark-Siders values in each of the girls. It was some sort of gene mutation that Raven got."

"So, that still didn't make her good." Another thought crossed my mind. "When did you go on vacation with them?"

As far back as I could remember Mr. McGurtle was always with Darla and me.

"Do you remember when Darla would take you to the beach during summer breaks?"

"Yes."

"That's when I'd go. It was sort of a break for me." He folded his hands in front of him. "I'm telling you, Raven is not the one who did this to her sister."

I wasn't going to buy it completely. There still wasn't an answer to why everyone in Whispering Falls was falling ill, and their spiritual gifts seemed to be disappearing. Nor did standing here discussing the good Mortimer sister against the bad Mortimer sister solve the issue of Eloise.

"This isn't helping matters." I walked over to the cauldron and picked up the spray bottle next to it. I smiled. "I bet Hili made me some of Izzy's cleaner," I whispered and sprayed the cauldron.

There was never a better time to get it good and clean as the beginning of a cure for Faith.

"More importantly," I threw in a pinch of sandlewood, and then Chamomilla to start the bubbling process. My intuition told me to even throw in some Eupbrasia/eyebright. With a handful thrown in, the swirling, watery tonic rose to a beautiful ivory color. Like the skin tone of Faith.

A good sign already. This lifted my spirits a little more, telling me that I was on the right path.

Chapter Twenty-Five

With a swing of the front door, Izzy, Gerald, Chandra, and Petunia bolted in the room. Each looking a little more under the weather then earlier.

"After talking with Mac," Izzy pointed to Mr. McGurtle, "We believe that whatever is going on at Hidden Hall is taking a toll on the entire spiritualist community. As the village President, I took it upon myself to contact other community Presidents. They are all reporting the same thing. Each shop is slowly losing its power and the shop owners have fallen ill."

"Just like us." Petunia coughed in the crook of her arm. Gerald reached over and patted her back.

"There has to be something you can do." Chandra leaned against the counter. Her strength getting weaker. "I wonder what's taking Oscar so long." She ran her hands up and down her cubby arms.

"Where is Oscar?" I begged to know.

"He was kind enough to run to Locust Grove to get some medicine." Gerald said, "You weren't here for a cure. And the intern *Dean Helena* sent was no good."

Ignoring his comment about Hili was best. They didn't know that Hili wasn't a potion maker, but was only here to help Oscar keep the shop in order. Although the ingredients were low, she seemed to do what she was sent to do. . .keep it in order.

It was just like Oscar to do what he could do. I only wished he'd hurry up.

"I know you are busy trying to find a cure for the Mortimer girl, but do you think you could do a quick smudging ceremony of purification for Whispering Falls?" Izzy's eyes dripped with worry. Wrinkles deep set between them.

"Of course I can." It was going to be a while before the potion was going to be done. A quick smudging ceremony could take place. "Go on up and I'll meet you there in five minutes."

I started to gather the ingredients before they left the shop. With sage and juniper as the main ingredients, I run up to the Gathering Rock as fast as I could to start the purification.

Everyone was gathered around, holding hands. Even Mr. Prince Charming stood at the foot of Izzy. They opened a little path for me to walk through. Carefully, I laid the ingredients on the Rock. The Rock was known for the cleansing spirit and this was why it was the gathering place for the village.

"White sage, sweet grass, root, and cedar." I wanted everyone to know what I was using in case anyone was allergic. We had this happen before and it didn't turn out all that good.

I rolled them in a bundle and lit it. The smoke rose quickly to the dark, gray sky. With the bundle in one hand and a peacock feather in the other, I walked around and fanned the smoke.

"WA KONNN TAAAWNKAAH.... WA KONNN TAAAWNKAAH.... WA KONNN TAAAWNKAAH.... WA KONNN TAAAWNKAAH...." I took a breath between each chant as I circled around everyone, focusing on the center part of their bodies. . . their heart.

I prayed the positive energy would focus on the good of Whispering Falls, the good of having Eloise in the village, and even the good of Faith Mortimer.

I laid the bundle on the Rock for it to smolder out. Walking over to the group, I felt a hand on my arm.

"Oscar." My heart soared when I looked into his blue eyes. Calmness filled my soul, telling me that everything was going to be okay, but it had to happen now.

Without a word, he reached for my hand and led me to the group. We all stood in a circle with our eyes closed. I was sure we were all praying for the same thing.

Oscar squeezed my hand. I opened my eyes.

"It's time to figure this out." There was a thin smile on his lips as he gestured toward the shop.

He knew we had to find a cure and standing here wasn't getting us there any quicker.

Quietly we left everyone standing around the Rock to wait for the bundle to completely burn out. I looked back as the smoke continued to roll up into the dull sky. For a brief moment, I saw a little ray of sunshine where the smoke hit the gray.

"We are going to figure this out." I realized I still had Oscar's hand in mine.

"Yes we are." He continued ahead, briefly stopping to run his free hand down the side of my face.

"Oh, Oscar," I whimpered under his touch.

He put his finger up to my lips. "Shh. We will have a lifetime to figure this out." He gestured between us. "That means you have to find a cure."

We made it back to the shop in silence. The cauldron was at a rolling boil when I went over to stir it.

"You better hurry up." A weak voice came from Madame Torres. "Time is wastin. . ."

I picked her up. "Madame Torres?"

A faint smile crossed her red lipstick stained mouth. Her eyes filled with tears. "Hurry, June."

This was one time I wished Madame Torres *had* made a smart-aleck comment. But she didn't. Slowly she faded into the depths of the glass ball.

Hurriedly, I grabbed the potion bottle from behind the counter that had a subdued glow. It was the one I need to put the potion in.

With the ladle, I poured the potion in the bottle. It was so bright when it when in, but dulled as it settled.

Setting the bottle aside, I reached for the spray bottle cleaner.

"Where did this come from?" I held the plastic spray bottle in the air and sniffed it. "Ahh…" The smell of my favorite chocolate swirled in my nose. It smelled exactly like Ding Dongs. I didn't recall the scent earlier. Probably because Mr. McGurtle had filled my head with all sorts of new ideas.

"Hili. I did a little digging on her." Oscar seemed a bit annoyed. "She was always so bossy, telling me what to do with the cures and how I needed to fix them."

I laughed.

"You know she's a perfectionist. And if something doesn't go her way she throws a little tantrum." He lifted a brow.

"She's a young girl. What do you expect?" I took a cloth and rubbed the inside. "This is the best stuff."

"I expected her to be a little more mature, but she wasn't." He handed me a stack of papers. UnHidden Hall newspapers to be exact.

"Where did you get these?" Frantically I thumbed through the stack that dated back to a few years ago.

There were things underlined, circled, crossed out, and some pictures even had mustaches on them.

"At Eloise's tree house." He shrugged. "That's where she said Dean Heal told her to stay. So I took her there on the first night."

My eyes grew the size of the full moon, my mouth dropped open.

"What?" He asked, pausing to examine the paper that I was looking at.

"I. . .um. . .had no idea she was staying at Eloise's." I dropped the papers on the table and shoved then toward him. As a matter of fact, I never even questioned where she stayed while she was here on her internship. I pointed to the headline. "Read it."

IMPOSTER: There is a Dark-Sider posing as a Good-Sider

It has come to my attention that there may be a Dark-Sider posing as a Good-Sider. This person is a rich spoiled brat who will do anything with her daddy's money to get what they want. This person has tried to buy off Good-Siders for the ULTIMATE Spell. The spell that only Good-Siders have and keep secret. . .for good or evil. . .

Watch your backs, Good-Siders.

"What does this prove?" He pushed it back.

"Now read this one." I handed him the next installment of the UnHidden Hall Chronicles.

IMPOSTER STRIKES AGAIN. . .

We are almost close to exposing the Dark-Sider that is posing as a Good-Sider. Only this time, they have made a misstep and have proven who they are.

She will stop at nothing to get her hands on the ULTIMATE Spell.

Watch your backs, Good-Siders!

The quickest way for me to figure out what the Ultimate spell was, was through Madame Torres.

"Madame Torres, what is the ultimate spell that only Good-Siders know?" I peered deep into the ball.

Flashes of lightning bolts radiated as if there was a storm brewing in the globe. Madame Torres had mustered up enough strength to come through when I needed her to.

"Death." Her voice cracked. The flashes continued to dart around the ball. There was no sign of Madame Torres. "Death is the one spell that Spiritualist cannot perform. The Good-Siders are the only spiritualists that know the ingredients for death."

Instantly, I realized that Faith was not dead, because the Dark-Sider didn't know the Ultimate Spell, and the Dark-Sider doing this needed to keep the one Good-Sider that might tell the secret alive.

But how did Eloise tie into this?

"I'm telling you Hili is a weirdo witch." He tossed it on the table. "I'm just saying that she's a little weird marking stuff out beans or berries, and then I found a boatload of these."

He handed over a small drawstring sack that contained a bunch of little red beans with black tips.

"She was always standing behind your partition, using that big cauldron." He pretended like he was stirring a pot. "When I asked her what she was doing, she told me to mind my own business. Then she'd say, 'I don't tell you how to arrest people, do I?'"

I grabbed the Magical Cures book off my counter and the pages flipped quickly as if I was turning them.

"What in the world?" Oscar walked backwards. "Are you doing that?"

Shrugging, I never looked up. I completely concentrated on the book.

The whirlwind above the book stopped. The pages stopped flipping and it was open to the picture glossary in the back. I had seen these beans before, but I couldn't remember what they were used for.

There was a picture of the exact bean. The Rosemary Pea. I scanned the page, reading all I could in that split second. I began to shake as I realized that this was the deadliest bean of all, if ingested in the right potion.

"Oh my God, I think this is the main ingredient in the Ultimate Spell!" Suddenly I felt feverish. I had been giving Hili all the information I knew. She had me believing that Raven was the one who was going around trying to harm Hidden Hall A Spiritualist University students and facility, when it was really her.

Hili had spent her time as an intern trying to duplicate the Ultimate Spell, but she couldn't.

"The cleaner?" I picked up the bottle and smelled the tip. Exactly what I liked. . .Ding Dongs. "She replaced Eloise's cleaner with a poison, and she knew I wanted one. And it smells exactly like Ding Dongs."

There was confusion written all over Oscar's face. It was an explanation I was going to have to tell him later. There was no time to dilly-dally.

I jumped up. The chair fell backwards and crashed to the ground. I grabbed my bag, put Madame Torres in, and flung it across my shoulders.

"What?" Oscar forcefully held me by my arms to stop me. "Where are you going, June?

"Oscar," I stared up at him. There was a fright so deep in my body, I couldn't stop shaking. "She is more than a weirdo. Hili is the one who tried to kill Faith. And I think she has Eloise somewhere."

"We have to stop her." He let go and ran out the door with me.

"Don't forget the potion." He held it in the air.

"It's poison!" I ran out the door and yelled over my shoulder, "Come on! I'll explain later!"

Without another word between us, I knew where Eloise was. My greatest fear was that I was too late.

"Please let her be safe." I begged to the heavens as we ran through the woods to get to Eloise's tree house.

Tree house.

Little by little, things began to add up in my head. Eloise lived in a tree house. She was banned from Whispering Falls for being a Fairiwick. Only the Good-Siders know the Ultimate spell. Hili took Eloise because as a Good-Sider, Eloise would know the spell. She hasn't killed Eloise because Hili needs the spell. Only Eloise doesn't know it.

I ran faster. Hili might not know the Ultimate Spell, but she could use other means to kill Eloise, if she hadn't done so already.

Once we got to her house, we bolted up the stairs that climbed the trunk of the tree, two-by-two, until we reached the top. The door was wide open and a cauldron was bubbling over. A plume of smoke hovered.

"Pine needles." I gasped as the smell from the copper pot twirled around me.

"Pine needles?" Oscar questioned.

"Yes. Hili was making a potion with Faith or Raven in mind." The words came spilled out of my mouth had a slight chill behind them. If my hunches were right, Hili would stop at nothing to get the spell. "Just like the cauldron cleaner smelled like Ding Dongs."

I had to hurry up and find Eloise. I had to stop Hili. She was more than just a caster. She had a lot of magic in that little prissy body of hers. But she didn't have the one thing she needed. . .a Good-Sider.

The last place I wanted to go was back to Hidden Hall, but if I didn't, I knew Aunt Helena, Faith, and Raven would be next. And then the demise of the entire Spiritualist community.

Oscar's jaw was clenched. He shook his head.

"I don't like this, June." He paced around the room with papers clutched in his hands as I scampered from door to door looking for Eloise.

She was nowhere to be found.

"You need to take a look at these." He grabbed me from my frantic tirade and held the papers in front of me.

To everyone who doesn't believe in the Dark-Siders, beware. I'm an ingredient away from discovering the Ultimate Spell, no thanks to a few Good-Siders. I've done it all on my own in the name of all Dark-Siders.

Follow me and I will take you into the new spiritual world where we will rule the world and create the justice that is due to us!

There was no time to waste. I took Madame Torres out of my bag.

"Show me Eloise." I commanded. Nothing happened. I yelled, "Show me Eloise, **NOW**!"

Madame Torres appeared, visibly shaken. She had streaks of black running down her face. "I'm sorry. I can't. There is an evil force blocking her from you." She swallowed hard. "I'm afraid there is an evil force taking over the spiritual world and. . ."

The ball went black.

"Madame Torres?" I frantically shook the ball. "Madame Torres!"

It was hopeless. Madame Torres was disappearing before my eyes and I couldn't help her.

Eloise. I put the last image of her shackled to the wall in my mind and concentrated. I searched the mental picture for anything and everything. All I could recall was the Mandrake flower she played with in her fingers.

"I've got it!" I screamed at Oscar and I ran out the door and down the steps. Without turning back, I could hear Oscar right behind me. "Eloise grows Mandrake flowers in her garden. She has to be there somewhere."

We ran down the cobblestone pathway, zipping past the array of colorful flowers that I, in the past, enjoyed pruning with Eloise, and straight back into the garden.

We stopped, and in a mad frenzy I screamed out, "Eloise! Eloise!"

Thump, thump.

"Did you hear that?" Oscar turned his head and we waited for the sound.

Thump, thump, thump.

Out of nowhere, Mr. Prince Charming dashed across the garden near the gazebo patio.

Meowl, meowl. He went underneath the table and made a complete circle before he sat down.

I ran over and took a closer look. There was an outline of a circle. A witch's circle.

"Is that a trap door?" Oscar bent down on his knees and began to knock on the wood. The boards were loose and he pulled one up, exposing a set of stairs.

"You stay here." Oscar grabbed my hand and squeezed. His eyes grew serious and still. "I'd never forgive myself if something happened to you."

"I can't let you go alone." I vehemently shook my head.

Without even thinking that Hili could be down there, Oscar held my hand and led me down the steps.

Letting go of my hand, Oscar looked back. We locked eyes. We knew that behind the wooden door, Eloise was going to be there. Hopefully alive.

"1,2,3." Oscar pushed.

"Eloise!" I pushed past him and ran over to her limp body lying on the dirt floor in the corner of the room.

I grabbed her and wrapped her up in my arms, exactly
the way I had done a few days ago when Helena had cast
her away.

"Go," She muttered. "Stop her from killing anyone."

"I can't." Tears whaled in my eyes. "I can't leave you
here like this."

"Oscar can help me." She used all the strength she had
to talk.

"June is not going anywhere without me." Oscar knelt
down beside us. He began working on getting the chains
off Eloise's wrists. "I'm not putting her in danger."

"You can't enter Hidden Hall unless you have
received an invitation from Helena." Her words were soft,
but they stung like daggers. "June must go alone. She has
the power to stop Hili from taking over the world."

"What do you mean?" I begged her to tell me.

"Once the spell gets into the Dark-Sider's hands, they
become the ruler of the Spiritual world. Kind of like an
Armageddon." Eloise trailed off, keeping her eyes closed.

"Eloise," I whispered, almost fearing her answer. "Are
you a Dark-Sider?"

Slowly she nodded, confirming my suspicion.

With my suspicions confirmed, there was no time to waste. Hili was already at Hidden Hall and casting evil spells all over. She was going to stop at nothing and no one to get the Ultimate Spell.

"You be careful." Oscar had already freed one wrist. He stood up. "I don't know what I'd do if you weren't in my life. I barely survived four days."

"I'll be safe." My heart was torn in two. One side ached to stay with Oscar, while the other side was in fear of what Hili was doing to the new world in which I lived. I put my fingers up to his lips. "I promise I will be back."

I couldn't bring myself to say anymore. It was just best if I left, while I still had the courage.

Mr. Prince Charming was waiting by the trap door when I emerged from the dungeon.

"It's up to us." I let Mr. Prince Charming take the lead. I rubbed the owl charm that dangled from my bracelet. It was time to make some very wise decisions. It was time to confront Hili.

Chapter Twenty-Six

There was no way I was going to be able to do it alone, nor did I want to. I tapped the sign that pointed toward the campus, exposing the pathway through the wheat field.

In a distance, a gray cloud hung over the campus area, even the always bright Once Upon a Time Library.

Mr. Prince Charming gave the all clear as his tail waved me to come on. He proceeded ahead of me to make sure the coast was clear as we made our way through the campus streets.

Everything was shut down. Closed off. Hili had definitely made her presence and what she was after known.

A cold breeze swept past my right ear, sending a spine chilling prickles up my leg.

"Who's there?" I demanded to know.

Out of nowhere, Gus appeared.

"Gus, I'm so glad you are here." I grabbed him by the arm, and pulled him closer. "Are you the one who keeps whizzing by me, creating that cool breeze?"

"Probably. Dean Helena wanted to keep close tabs on you. You have come just in time. The students are on lockdown. Dean Helena is keeping watch over Faith. She knew you'd be back, so she revoked your expulsion." He glanced over to the Dark-Sider's edge of town. "It's the evil versus evil."

"Hili?" I feared.

"And Raven." He continued to look into the distance. He turned and looked at me. Panic rioted his face. "I'm scared. Raven can't beat Hili alone."

Meowl, meowl.

Mr. Prince Charming ran as fast as he could toward the Dark-Sider's part of town, disappearing into the woods. I ran after him, as I felt Gus teleporting past me.

"The good Dark-Sider has to win," His whispers were heard in the wind. "She has to save her sister."

I had to get to Raven. All this time she had been trying to save her sister.

Sigh. I inhaled as my intuition started to kick in. "Welcome back," I whispered.

"Yeah, welcome back," sarcasm dripped in his voice.

"I wasn't talking about me coming back here. My intuition seems to be back." I stopped just inside of the Dark-Siders territory. "Are you coming?"

"I can't." And he was gone.

There was no time to wait. Whispering Falls was dying by the second, all because of Hili. If Raven and I could join forces, maybe we had a shot at bringing the spiritualist world back.

Steam rolled out of Raven's tree-house windows. Unlike the last time I was here. My calves ached as I ran up the stairs as fast as I could. The door was wide open, and Raven was frantically stirring the cauldron with a long oar. Her long black hair was no longer lush. It had fallen in strings, swinging back and forth with each circle she created in the boiling potion.

The overwhelming smell of pinecones shot up my nose, making me gasp for air.

"What are you doing here?" She ground the words between her teeth. She was seething mad. Her tamed black straight hair was mussed up. Her dark eyes were set back in the deep black circles that formed around her eye sockets. "I can do this without your help."

"No you can't." I walked in and took the Magical Cures book from my purse. I held it up. "We can put our spiritual gifts together and bring Faith back."

"You fool!" She whipped around; her icy fingers taking hold of my forearm. "It's not Faith I'm worried about. It's us. The entire world will be destroyed if Hili has anything to do with it. Faith knew it was Hili. She was willing to sacrifice her life for me to save our family, our spiritualist community."

"Like a spiritualist martyr?" If only my intuition had worked while I was at University from the get-go, maybe this whole situation could've been stopped.

Raven slowly nodded without looking at me.

Without hesitation, I concentrated on the book looking for any and all cures that would help reverse the spell that Hili had cast on Faith. I had never reversed a potion, much less a cast.

"There is something that I'm missing and I don't know what." Raven's lack of sleep was beginning to show on her pale skin. She was beginning to look like Faith. "If Hili comes up with a potion or spell that will kill Faith, she will win and destroy us. Of course I want my sister back, but stopping Hili will help us win the war."

"I don't understand." There were so many things that didn't add up.

Raven viciously stirred the cauldron, her hair swooshing from side-to-side. "When Faith figured out that Hili was really a Dark-Sider, she started to talk about the Ultimate Spell. Hili was unable to really talk about it because Dark-Siders don't know the spell. *I* don't know the spell." She threw in a dash of Eyebright. The elixir turned amethyst with copper accretions on the side. The pinecone smell turned to the aroma of coffee. The moving liquid glowed, and then turned to brown.

The Magical Cures Book opened to a page on its own. I stepped back, realizing this was a new power I had. I didn't know anything about Telekinesis, but I was going to use everything I could.

I concentrated on Faith lying in the bed. My intuition told me to really focus on the fingernails and her lungs that I had already brought back to life.

"Where is Hili?" I asked. Swiftly the turning pages created a wind, blowing my bangs back.

"I don't know." Raven didn't stop. She no longer stirred in nice, neat circle. She used the oar erratically, causing the potion to tumble over the sides. "I cast a spell around the perimeter of the Dark-Siders village that won't allow Teletransporter's to enter."

No wonder Gus couldn't come.

"Wait." I put my hand in the air. "Hili is a Teletransporter?"

"Yes, among other things." Raven let go of the oar, but the oar continued to rotate. Sweat was pouring down her face. "I'm just in my first year of University. I have no idea what I'm doing. Hili has taken over the entire campus."

"I think I know where I can find her." I looked down when the Magical Cures Book stopped. "Here, this is what you need to add. You need to help your sister."

"Thank you, June." Raven slumped into my arms, giving a gentle squeeze. "Where are you going?"

"I'm going to find Hili."

I left as quickly as I had come. Mr. Prince Charming darted ahead of me to make sure the coast was clear. The street was still empty and the grey cloud was looming closer. Magic hung in the air, and it wasn't a good form of magic.

The cottage dorm was dark and the door was pushed open. Little puffs of smoke wafted from the light fixtures as if someone had burned them. Mr. Prince Charming and I climbed the stairs.

The framed, retired professors' eyes all smoldered with fire.

Hiss, hiss. Mr. Prince Charming arched his back at the top of the stairs. His body turned toward the hallway. Our hallway. Faith's, Hili's and mine.

The door to Hili's room was wide open. All the photographs on her wall flickered in the light of the lit candles. I remember exactly what she said to me the first day I stepped in her room and looked at those pictures.

"That's my daddy. He wants me to be really successful in school."

I had a feeling her daddy didn't want her to be notoriously successful as the Jeffery Dahmer of the Spiritual world.

A shadow cast down the wall, catching my attention, I jumped, turning around.

"I wondered how long it was going to take you to come back." Hili was no longer dressed in her cute little Capri's and matching tops. She was wearing a black cape with a pointy collar. She had dyed her blond hair coal black. She peeled off the long black gloves, finger-by-finger. "What? Never seen a dark witch before? Oh honey, my little princess act was just that. An act!"

Slowly I backed up and found the wall behind me.

"It took everything I had not to dive into your delicious little Oscar." A thunderous laugh left her body. "I don't have time for a wannabe sorcerer. You should've seen his little wand. Pit.I.Ful."

There was a desire in her eyes, as she looked me up and down. I stood, waiting for my intuition to kick in.

Please don't fail me now.

"Umm…June, you shouldn't leave a man like that alone in this big bad spiritual world." She walked past me and abruptly turned back around. "Any girl would gobble him up. Including me."

She opened the door that I had tried to open when I first visited her room. What a fool I was. *Some intuition I had.*

The room was filled with shelves of potion bottles, and a big cauldron sat in the middle. UnHidden Hall Chronicles were stacked in the corner.

I remembered how she stopped me from opening the door because she was "*too embarrassed for you to see my messy closet.*"

"What? You think that I was going to let you in on my little secret just because you are the Dean's niece?" She scoffed. "You are no threat to me. You are old. Your man on the other hand is just my type. So mark my words, when I do away with all of you, I'll go back and get him for myself." An evil grin crossed her lips, exposing her pointy eyeteeth. "Honey, we young girls love older men."

She pulled out an ingredient from underneath her cloak and dropped it in the boiling cauldron, sending the calm potion into a fury. Sparks flew everywhere.

"What was that?" Anger boiled in me, but I had to keep my calm. Hili was on the edge and she was completely insane.

Laughing, she walked back with her fingers outstretched, pushing me down onto the couch. Suddenly her eyes held an eager evilness. Something I had never seen before. Something that frightened me to my core.

"It's time to do away with you June Heal, and all of Hidden Hall. Any last requests?"

"Why? Why are you doing this? Why did you hurt Faith?"

"Those are easy questions to answer." She drummed her fingers together while she paced back and forth in front of me. "I was only curious to find out what the Ultimate Spell was made of, so I pretended to be a Good-Sider. That was when Little Miss Prissy Pants started to dig around."

As she turned to back, my eyes darted around the room looking for anything to hit her over the head with and knock her out. Somehow, I had to get her tied up. Just like she had done Eloise.

Why? Why couldn't I have any cool magical abilities? Like turning her into a beetle so I could step on her and squish her. There was no sense in asking such fruitless questions now.

Hili continued, waving her hands in the air as sparks flew from her fingertips. I ducked; making sure none of them hit me. Her voice escalated, "I warned her not to come clean with any of it, but she refused. She gave me what she called 'time to change,' but there was no changing. I sick and tired of being on the wrong side." She tilted her head from side-to-side and rolled her eyes. "Change? She or you have no idea what it's like to be an outcast among your peers all of your life. I'm going to make a change when I have the Ultimate Spell in my hands. The Dark-Siders will rule the world!"

Her words stung. I concentrated on the pictures of her family hanging on the wall. *Was this the success your father wanted?* I wanted to ask, but kept my mouth shut. Time. I needed to buy some more time to figure something out.

"What spell did you cast to put her in a deep sleeping coma?" This was one thing I couldn't figure out.

"No, no, no." She took the ripped out page from the Mortimer file off her desk and threw it at me. I quickly glanced down at it:

Remember that Faith has very special powers. She made the Ultimate Spell at the age of three without ever touching on her spiritual gifts. And it could be very dangerous if anyone knew about this.

Please, Faith is extremely allergic to Rosemary Pea and it can kill her. Some potions call for it, but unfortunately her love of pine cones overshadow her innate ability Faith has to know the ingredient is in the potion.

As for Raven, she is a sweet Dark-Sider. Her mother and I have learned everything we can about the Dark-Sider community. Raven has attended the prestigious Pitch-Black Academy. She's completely aware of her amazing powers of having some Good-Sider traits.

We'd appreciate it if you could keep it quiet that Faith and Raven are sisters. This is due to the fact that they want to set their own ways in life. They had decided at an early age to respect each other's lot in life.

She snatched the note from my fingertips.

"I don't care about Raven. She's nothing. But I care about the Ultimate Spell and taking over the spiritual world." She neatly folded the page and stuck it on the desk. Her eyes were hooded like a hawk. "You have no idea what I'm going to do when I rule the world."

"That's the problem. If you try to do the spell, you will destroy the spiritual world, not just the one you live in." The words left my mouth, as I searched my mind for any intuitive inkling left in my body. I was fresh out of intuitive notions. Maybe some quick talking common sense would kick in.

"Unfortunately for you, I'm willing to take that chance." Her brows drew together in an angry frown. "I'm a very quick Teletransporter. Since Faith was allergic to the Rosary Pea, I quickly slipped in the ladle after she pushed you aside like a mutt during Intuition Class when your ever-so-wonderful Eloise offered you the sleeping potion. Just like I added a little Rosemary Pea to Eloise's cleaner."

Hili moved around the room in swift motions. Never once did I take my eyes off her.

"It really is a shame, for a moment I really did believe that you and I could be friends."

"Yeah, well this little stunt proves we can't." I made the crazy sign with my finger.

"Oh shut up!" She bent down and pressed her pointy little nose to my nose. "You are nothing but a little psychic."

She straightened up and pranced to the other side of the room.

"My daddy always said I was going to leave a mark on this world." She brushed her hand along the picture of the two them framed on her wall that I had been concentrating on.

"How did Eloise fit into your grand scheme of things?" There had to be some way to outwit her. A white flash caught my attention. Without moving my head, I looked out of the corner of my eye. Mr. Prince Charming was doing figure eights around someone that I couldn't see.

Gus. Instantly, I felt much better knowing that he was there. He had to be teletransporting back and forth between

Aunt Helena and me, giving her updates on what Hili was doing.

"For a professor, she really isn't that smart." Hili firmly planted her hand on her hip, while she flailed the other one about. "I guess you heard that your precious little professor is really---Just. Like. Me." She shot me a twisted smile.

She reached beneath her cape and suddenly it appeared.

"Jeez!" I held my hands in air and tried to press myself up against the back of the couch to make a little more room between me and Hili's magic. . .gun.

"Oh, yeah." She waved it around like it was her casting wand. "This is my magic. I might not be able to find out the real Ultimate Spell, but this ultimate guy will do the job."

Out of the corner of my eye I could see a faint light coming from my bag. *Madame Torres?*

My heart jumped, thinking that the spell Hili had performed on the magical world was dissolving and coming to an end. After all, she really wasn't that powerful yet and her spells were just temporary. But she could do a lot of damage in *that* temporary amount of time.

"I'm going to check my potion. Now, don't you go anywhere." She aimed the gun straight at my forehead with smug delight. "Don't you try to go running off, because I will use this little tool of magic."

She disappeared into the small room.

Quickly I pulled my purse to me and grabbed for whatever was glowing. It was the extra bottle of protective potion that I had made for Faith.

In a split second, I screwed off the top and threw it at Hili as soon as she walked back into the room.

"What are you doing?" She stormed over with the gun pointing at me. The potion spilled out of the bottle in mid-air and sprayed all over her, just as the picture I had been concentrating on flew off the wall and smashed into her side temple.

A gun shot rang out.

The blast was so loud that I raised my hands up to my cover my ears from the pain. Only it wasn't pain from the noise that I felt, it was from the blood gushing out of my arm. That was the last thing I remember.

Chapter Twenty-Seven

"June? June?" The sweetest voice besides Darla's that I had ever heard, called for me to open my eyes. "I think she's coming to."

Slowly I let light creep in between the creases of my lids and let them adjust until I could fully open them.

"Her eyes are open." Oscar shielded the glare of the overhead lights; his smile was from ear to ear. He leaned down and whispered in my ear, "I'm so glad you came back to me."

I started to talk, but my mouth was dry.

"Don't. Anything we have to say can wait." His lips brushed against my ear, and his words wrapped around me like a warm blanket. "I just want you to get better so I can take you home."

Slowly I nodded and blinked, letting him know I felt the same way.

"Thank you, Oscar." Mr. McGurtle stood at the foot of my hospital bed. "After the little gunshot wound to your arm, I was afraid you were a goner. But with a little nudging from the Dean, she let Oscar come."

Aunt Helena stood on the other side of my bed. There was satisfaction on her face. She reached down and brushed my bangs down with her long fingernails. "Yes, Oscar will have to come to school too. But I think I'll let Mac give him private sorcerer lessons until you are all better."

I had forgotten about the gunshot and most of what had happened with Hili, but the more awake I became, the more I remembered.

I reached for Oscar.

"Is Eloise okay?" I asked. He touched my trembling lips with one finger.

"Everyone is great. You did it." He leaned down. His lips touched mine like a secret whisper.

Beeep, beep, beeeeep.

The monitor reflected the thumping of my heart.

"Okay you two." The doctor came in and made his way in between Oscar and me. "You have plenty of time to do all that when Ms. Heal is out of here."

There was collective laughter throughout the room. Even I let out a little laugh. Oscar's sweet kiss was exactly the cure I needed to get well.

The doctor did a couple more vital tests before he told us that I was free to go home.

"Home as in Whispering Falls?" Or was I going to have to stay at Hidden Hall and finish up my last couple of days?

"Yes, Whispering Falls." The doctor shuffled out of the room

"So Hili didn't figure out the Ultimate Spell?" My eyes darted around the room, taking in everyone's expression.

"No. You killed her." Aunt Helena's expression grew still. Just like the rest of the room. "Don't you remember?"

I shook my head. The last thing I did remember was the blood dripping down my arm and hitting my shoe.

"You hit her over the head with the picture frame." Mr. McGurtle seemed to know all the details. "How did you get to the picture frame anyways?"

Mewl, Mewl. Mr. Prince Charming lifted his head off my pillow. Our eyes met. He knew as well as I did that my new power killed Hili. A new power I was going to keep under wrap until I knew how to really use it.

"Let's just say she's pretty quick with her hands." Gus responded to the question, letting me off the hook.

"No matter what you did, it saved our lives." Faith's faint but steady voice called across the room.

Oscar moved and the entire room came into focus. Faith and I were sharing a room in the Hidden Hall hospital.

Raven gave a slight wave from the other side of her sister.

"I used the potion from your book, and it brought her right back to life." Raven walked over with the Magical Cures Book in her hand. She laid it on the bedside table. "I can never thank you enough."

"Or me," Faith whispered in the background before she closed her eyes to take a catnap.

"Seriously, one day you have to tell me what happened in the cottage dorm." Raven reached down and squeezed my hand. "After all, we are going to be running a shop in the same village."

Chapter Twenty-Eight

"This would've never happened if I was the Dean." Gerald said with a smug look on his face as he twisted his mustache around with his fingers.

"Well, you aren't." Aunt Helena scoffed back just before the Whispering Falls Grand Re-Opening Parade started down Main Street. Her scar grew a burnt red.

After the stunt Hili had pulled on the spiritualist world, it caused business to go downhill. The lush Kentucky bluegrass had burnt up, but with the help of some new spiritualists in town and a chant or two, the grass was greener than ever.

We had to find a way to bring visitors back to our little spiritual world in Kentucky. With a new shop in town, and everyone feeling their best, we knew a grand reopening would bring the customers in masses. And it worked.

Main Street was lined with some customer faces I recognized and some I didn't. There were already lines formed in front of every single store, including A Charming Cure.

"What do you mean?" I asked Gerald as he helped me into the back of the green machine. When they asked me to be the Grand Marshal of the parade, I asked Gerald to drive for me since he loved the green machine as much as I did.

"This grand reopening, because I would've stopped Hili before she let the communities get in a state where we had to battle back." He took his top hat off and threw it on the ground.

"You listen here you old geezer!" Aunt Helena's cloak flew open and her finger flew out, sharply pointed at Gerald's head. "It's about time I make it even after all these years."

"Don't you think you made it even enough?" Gerald smacked her hand away, just as a spark flew from it and hit the window of Belle's Baubles.

"Stop it" Belle screamed, running out of her shop, exposing the space between her two front teeth. She planted her legs apart with each arm outstretched. Aunt Helena on one side, Gerald on the other. "I knew this day would come. But this is a joyous day. Can't we all get along? Haven't we all been through enough?"

I got off my perch in the back of the green machine, and jumped out.

"Let's bury our differences for once and for all." I begged the two of them. "Exactly what is this all about?"

Hiss, hiss. Mr. Prince Charming batted at Aunt Helena.

"You too!" I pointed at him.

Meow, meow. He did figure eights around my ankle. In the distance I could see Oscar clearing the street so the parade could start. I wasn't sure how much longer he was going to be able to hold off the big crowd. Plus, I was anxious to get back to my life.

"Your Aunt and I were once. . ." Gerald cleared his throat, "an item. After I found out she was going to be going to Hidden Hall A Spiritualist University as the Dean, I became a little upset."

"A little?" Aunt Helena leaned in. The scar on her face was the reddest I had ever seen it. She ran a finger down it. "Do you see this?"

Oh my! Excitement built up inside me. Was I finally going to learn how she got that scar?

"Yes."

"He gave me the wrong direction to Hidden Hall on purpose and I was jumped by a Dark-Sider who wanted me to give him the Ultimate Spell. He cut me and left me for dead!" She drew her cloak around her.

"But I found you and you were okay." Gerald sighed with exasperation. "As a matter of fact, because of it, I was banned to perform any magic other than tea leaf reading."

"You deserved it!" Aunt Helena didn't take her eyes off him and stomped her red-heeled thigh high boot on his top hat.

"You!" He shook his fist at her.

But her look was distant as if she was thinking about the accident.

I leaned in and whispered, "Are you okay?"

"He's out there somewhere. "Her gaze broke, her face clouded with uneasiness. "I'm waiting for the day to avenge what he did to me."

"That was forty years ago. Can we please move on?" Belle pushed her long blond hair behind her shoulders and put her arms back down to her side. She looked between the two of them. "Okay?"

"Fine." Gerald picked up his hat and shook out the crease Aunt Helena's boot had made.

"Fine." Aunt Helena folded her arms across her chest and turned away from him, giving him the cold shoulder.

Without another word, Gerald offered me a hand to get back in the bed of the green machine. Oscar started the sirens on his police car. It was time to throw out the big bucket of candy to all the customers waiting for the magic of Whispering Falls to come into their lives.

"Oh get away." Aunt Helena stomped as Mr. Prince Charming did figure eights around her ankles. "I'm in no mood to forgive two people in one day."

I couldn't help but chuckle. No one could refuse the charm of Mr. Prince Charming.

With the parade underway, I waved and threw out candy to everyone.

"Over here!" The children called out for me to throw candy their way. "Over here!"

I waved and tossed it out as quickly as I could. With each passing face, I could already tell which customers were going to visit A Charming Cure for whatever ailed them. There were some with heartache, money troubles, joint pain, and secrets. I was ready. I was ready to get back to my life of helping people fix what they didn't even know was wrong with them. And keep them coming back for more.

A dark shadowy figure caught my eye when I was scanning the crowd. When I looked back to find the figure, it was gone.

My mind recalled the first week I moved to Whispering Falls, I had seen that same shadowy figure in the street right in front of Gollybee Pet Store. Recently I saw the figure near the Gathering Rock.

Was someone keeping tabs on me?

I shook the notion. Whispering Falls was filled with all sorts of characters. It could have been anyone.

"Come by when you are done!" Raven shouted from her new shop in town, Wicked Good Bakery. Her long black hair was beautifully pulled up in a neat ponytail that hung over her left shoulder. She wiped her hands down her baking apron that had the Wicked Good logo printed on the front. "I've got a surprise for you."

"Great! I love surprises!" I shouted back and threw her a wad of candy from my candy bucket. Only it hit the stripped blue and pink awning that hung just above the hot pink ornamental wooden door, and then landed in the cupcake in her hand. "Oops! I never said I was a good throw."

She shook her head before waving back and disappearing into her new shop. The new shop that was right next door to The Gathering Grove.

"I guess you won't need the green machine to go into the bakery in Locust Grove." I shouted into the window of my old El Camino. Gerald could contract with Raven and they'd do a great business together.

"Oh, we do for the ingredients," he shouted back. "Remember, there's not a grocery store in Whispering Falls. . . yet!"

Yet. That always seemed to be the answer. . . yet.

I continued to wave as the Grand Marshal of our short little trip down Main Street. I looked behind me, noticing all the other shop owners waving to the crowd as well.

Whispering Falls was back to our normal, happy, magical community. My soul sighed with delight as the bright warm sun beat down on my uplifted face.

Even the Karima sisters were behaving. Most of the time they were running around trying to assess the health status of customers and spiritualists, with a secret hope that their funeral business was going to pick up soon.

"Hear ye, hear ye, and read all about the Grand Reopening in tomorrow's edition of Whispering Falls Chronicles." The voice rang above the crowd, catching my attention. "Whispers can be loud if you listen closely!"

A hand waved a newspaper above the heads of the crowd. I continued to wave as I watched for on opening in the people to see who the hand belong to.

"Hear ye, hear ye." There was a little opening right before A Charming Cure. "Get your first edition of The Whispering Falls Chronicles."

My mouth dropped when Faith Mortimer appeared, profusely waving the paper in the air. Her long blonde hair was long gone into a short razor cut, almost completely covered by a pageboy hat.

"Hi, June!" She ran over and threw a paper in the bed of the green machine. "Enjoy!"

I picked up the paper and the headlines read: Wicked Good Bakery now open on Main Street, and Whispering Falls Isn't Whispering About The New Newspaper In Town.

There couldn't be a better addition to the community than the Mortimer sisters. They were welcomed with open arms.

We pulled back around to stop where we had started. In front of Belle's Baubles.

"Thank you, Sir." I took Gerald's hand getting out of the back of the green machine. "You were a very good escort."

"Why, you are so welcome." He did a little bow. "Would you like a spot of tea before you head to man the big line outside of A Charming Cure?"

We looked down the street. Not only did A Charming Cure have a line, but every single shop did. Even Wicked Good.

"You know what." I held my hand in the air. "I think I'll take a rain check. There's someone I need to see."

I ran across the street, noticing Faith was already taking pictures and jotting some notes on her journalist pad. Her new job suited her. And she looked very happy and healthy.

"Wow," the word popped out of my mouth as I pushed the big pink wooden door open and walked inside Wicked Good.

The lime green walls looked amazing against the jars of candy that lined them. The cake stands on each table had the most amazing assortment of cupcakes I'd ever seen.

The black and white checker floor lead the way to a room filled with Victorian style dining furniture. The menu had any dessert you could ask for as well as any tea that was sold at the Gathering Grove.

"So?" Raven snuck up behind me. Her hands were behind her back. "What do you think?"

"I. . ." The words were stuck. "I'm shocked. It's amazing." I ran my hand along the old Victorian tables she had rehabbed in an off-white finish. "Beautiful, Raven. Absolutely beautiful."

She brought her hands in front of her. "Today's special, June's Gem." There was a chocolaty round treat on the plate in her hand.

"Is that what I think it is?" My mouth watered at the thought of a homemade Ding Dong.

"Try it." Her eyes glistened. "In honor of you."

Carefully I took the yummy goodness off the plate and bringing it up to my nose, I took a sniff.

"Umm..." I closed my eyes to enjoy every single smell. Splitting it in two, I handed Raven half. "Here's to us."

"Ding Dong, the witch is dead." Laughing out loud, we tapped our two halves together before we devoured every single morsel.

"Yes, the witch is dead." I knew my smile was filled with chocolate teeth. "This is amazing."

I followed Raven back up to the front of Wicked Good. She handed me a box of June's Gems.

"I must go. My customers wait." I gave her a quick hug and headed toward A Charming Cure, Mr. Prince Charming next to me the whole way, his tail wagging in the air.

My heart filled seeing Belle's Baubles overflowing with customers. Bella looked out the window and winked before she buried her head back in the jewelry case.

Across the street, customers were in a line to get a table at The Gathering Grove Tea Shoppe. I was sure Gerald was already reading someone's tea leaves.

"Excuse me." I barely missed a collision with a man carrying a very large crystal chandelier out of Mystic Lights.

"I smell death." Constance Karima rushed past me with her twin sister, Patience, on her heels. Both dressed in housecoats, they hurried along.

"Yes, death." Patience repeated after her sister. *Death?*

But, quickly dismissed the notion when a kangaroo hopped out of Glorybee Pet Store and Petunia running after it flailing her arms in the air.

I ran as fast as I could to cut the joey off at the pass, but Mr. Prince Charming had already come face-to-face with it, stopping the kangaroo dead in its tracks.

"Gotcha!" Petunia pushed a few of the leaves that were dangling from her messy up-do back in place. "I hate it when good souls come back as an animal they do not want to be. At least you came back to life," she scolded the animal after grabbing it up.

Before I reached A Charming Cure, I peeked my head into A Cleansing Spirit Spa.

"You are going to make a fantastic mother," Chandra chuckled and rubbed the palm of the young woman sitting at the manicure table in front of her. "Oh, twins too!"

"How did you know?" The woman let out a cry of joy. "The only other person that knows is my husband."

"Honey, I can see it in your hands." Chandra glanced up at me with a twinkle in her eye that matched the sparkle on the gem in the center of her turban.

I waved and skipped next door to open A Charming Cure.

Chapter Twenty-Nine

"Welcome to A Charming Cure." I greeted each customer that came in.

"I was in here a couple of days ago. You gave me a cure for my acne." The blonde reminded me of her visit only a few short days ago, but it seemed like a lifetime had happened since then. "I wanted to thank you. It was gone by the time I got home. It was like. . ." She searched for a word.'

"Magic."

"Yes. Magic." She turned and began looking around the shop. Fortunately, nothing she needed jumped out at me, or better yet, at my intuition.

But the young man standing in the corner of the bath salts did grab my attention.

"Can I help you?" I asked the bewildered gentleman who had a distant look on his face.

Bouncing on the balls of his feet, his curly red head jiggled, a little bit like Bozo the Clown. "I. . .um. . .have a little problem." He glanced down toward his nether region.

"Oh. . ." I stammered, feeling a little flushed.

He leaned in. "I heard you might be able to help. I mean, homeopathic cures are like the new thing. Right?" Worry set deep in his eyes.

"Yes." I rubbed my hands down my apron, and clasped my hands together. "I think I might have exactly what you need. I'll be right back."

This was a new one to me, and very exciting.

The cauldron was ready to go. I grabbed some Ginseng, L argentine and Gingko Biloba off the ingredient shelf, along with a pinch of banana peel, salmon, and pine nuts. Carefully I stirred each ingredient in, focusing on my customer's sexual desire.

There was a little something missing. I peeked around the petition and grabbed the gentleman's attention. I waved him over.

"Do you have a picture of your significant other?" I asked knowing it was a strange question.

He didn't question me; he pulled his wallet out of his back pocket and retrieved a wedding picture of a woman with the same colored hair as him. "It was our wedding day. She's lovely."

The pride swelled on his face, never taking his eyes off her as he handed me the photo. Without warning, I tossed it in the cauldron. His eyes grew big.

"It'll be done in a few." I planted a grin on my face and disappeared back over the cauldron.

The indigo potion reflected against the copper cauldron sending out gold flashes. The elixir whirled and twirled, causing a small funnel cloud about one inch above the glowing tonic. It thickened with each stir of the oar, causing the cloud to go slower and slower until it disappeared into the air.

The masculine cobalt blue empty potion bottle lit up behind me, letting me know it was the right bottle for this man's. . .little issue.

With the golden lid unscrewed, I plunged the bottle into the cauldron, allowing it to fill to the top. I wanted to make sure he used every single ounce.

The smell of bagels engulfed my senses. Screwing the lid back on, his potion was complete and his problem would soon be gone.

"Here you go." I held the beautiful masculine bottle out when I found him in the crowd. "You need to sprinkle a couple dashes on your bagel every morning."

He held the bottle up to the light. The thick mixture had turned to a fine grain, the size of salt.

"Oh, if your wife mistakes it for salt, it won't affect her in any way." I winked. "Only you."

We walked back to the cash register to make good on what he owed me.

Ding, ding. The bell above the door dinged, but I didn't know how another customer was going to fit into the store. It was filled beyond fire code.

Aunt Helena tipped her head back when I looked up. I couldn't help but wonder what she wanted of me now that all the drama was over. We never seemed to see eye-to-eye, but I guess that was most families. Just not mine.

Her face caught a light that brought back a memory of an image that was buried deep in my mind. Only in the memory she didn't have her scar, she held out a doll. In the memory, a young girl took it. The young girl was me, standing next to my dad's coffin.

Our eyes held for a minute and she knew. She knew exactly what I remembered.

Without a word spoken about it, she walked up to the counter.

"I'm glad to see business doing so well." She glanced around the room. "I have a present for you before I go back to Hidden Hall."

She put a brown paper bag on the counter. I unrolled the top and reached in, pulling out an old photo of Darla, my father, and me standing in front of my cottage on the hill.

"Thank you." I reached out to hug my aunt, but she was gone. I held the frame close to my heart and hugged it. It was the only picture I have of my family. Darla always told me that memories were kept in your heart. But it was nice to have the real thing.

I studied how happy we looked and wondered what they would've thought of my life and how it turned out. I couldn't wait to hang it up. It was going to stay in the shop, where I spend most of my time.

Throughout the day, I found myself glancing at the picture and smiling. My intuition told me that they approved of how things were turning out.

"Are you ready?" I rubbed my hand down Mr. Prince Charming's back, while looking out the front window of the shop wondering why Oscar hadn't stopped by.

There was a strange gnawing in my gut that made me question whether or not Oscar had changed his mind. Was he keeping his distance so he didn't have to face the embarrassment of having kissed me in the hospital? Was it a spur of the moment kind of thing?"

Tapping each bottle of ingredients before I left, I took another look around my shop.

"Well, Darla," I walked over to the picture that Aunt Helena had given me of my parents. My finger slide down the face of my mother and I stopped on her lips. I didn't remember my father's voice, but I remember Darla's. Suddenly I wished I could hear her voice just one more time. "How do you think I turned out?"

Madame Torres lit up and I turned to see what smart-aleck thing was going to come out of her mouth. She wasn't the sentimental type and tried to make me laugh when I was.

"Proud," The voice that came out of the crystal ball sounded just like Darla.

"Madame Torres, that's not funny." I walked over and peered deep into the ball.

"Oh, June." My parents stood inside Madame Torres with their arms around each other. Darla grinned. "We are so proud of you. Keep listening to your amazing intuition. We love you."

Before I could answer, they faded away. Tears filled my eyes as more and more memories of my family flooded my mind.

"They are only a wish away." Madame Torres appeared. There was even a tear in her eye.

Well, if I didn't have Oscar, I at least had my parents.

"Alright. Time for bed." I picked up Madame Torres, the box of June's Gems and locked A Charming Cure behind us.

Tomorrow was another day that was going to be rewarding, providing people with the cures for what really ailed them.

The dark night sky took me off-guard. I hadn't left the shop all day, and the bright full moon let me know that.

The fireflies darted about, teasing Mr. Prince Charming as we made our way back to our little cottage on the hill.

"Darn teenagers." I laughed, watching Mr. Prince Charming bat a few of them down.

A flying spark in the distance caught my eye. I followed the flicker all the way to the Rock.

Just as I was hypnotized by his kiss, the sight of him had an even greater hold on me. A smile crossed my face as I watched him try to cast with his wand and nothing but a spark came about.

A twig broke underneath my shoe, exposing my presence.

A vaguely sensuous light passed between us as our eyes met. It was the first time we were alone since. . .the kiss.

Chapter Thirty

"How did your first day back go?" Oscar put the wand in the pocket of his pants as if he wasn't practicing.

"Busy." Cautiously I walked up, looking for any sign of rejection.

Maybe it was the magic in the air, or a true desire, but I couldn't help but replay how soft his lips felt against mine.

"You look like you're back to normal." He shuffled his feet, his blue eyes meeting mine. "I wanted to give you time to heal, and change your mind if you wanted to."

"Change my mind?" The closer I got, I was sure he could hear my heart that was about to beat right out of my chest.

He grabbed the box of June's Gems out of my hand and placed it on the Rock. He turned my palm over and ran a finger along the lines.

"It doesn't take a palm reader to tell that a very dark, handsome policeman is going to take up a big space in your heart." He pulled my palm up to his lips. The heat felt like his lips were tattooed on my palm.

Meow, meow.

He glanced at Mr. Prince Charming, and then back at my palm. "The other side of that heart is taken up by an ornery white cat."

My emotions whirled as he swept me weightless into his arms, claiming my lips for his own.

His wand bounced out of his pocket and shot up in the air creating the biggest spark I had ever seen.

Pulling away, we watched the spark fly into the sky, bursting into a display of the most amazing fireworks, blanketing the entire town of Whispering Falls.

"Welcome home, June Heal."

I snuggled against him, thinking about the words he had just spoken.

Home.

Yes, his arms felt exactly like home.

"Why do I have to sit here and watch this?" Madame Torres groaned from my bag. "Can't you take me home, and then. . ."

Oscar stuck my bag in the tall grass, muffling my snarky crystal ball before he took me right back into his arms, giving me a kiss that melted my tired soul.

About The Author

International bestselling author Tonya Kappes spends her day lost in the world of her quirky characters that get into even quirkier situations.

When she isn't writing, she's busy being the princess, queen and jester of her domain which includes her BFF husband, her teenage guys, two dogs, and one lazy Kitty.

Tonya has an amazing STREET TEAM where she connects with her fans on a daily basis. If you are interested in becoming a Tonya Kappes Street Team member, be sure to message her on Facebook.

For more information, check out Tonya's website, Tonyakappes.blogspot.com.

CPSIA information can be obtained at www.ICGtesting.com
Printed in the USA
LVOW080917171212

312006LV00001B/71/P